OCT 3 0 1997

THE STREET SINGERS OF LUCKNOW
and Other Stories

urratulain Hyder is one of the leading writers of India and a recipient
f the country's highest literary honour, the Jnanpith Award.

act, fantasy, and trenchant satirical humour, diligent research and
omantic imagination, baroque pastiche and clipped post-modernism
ombine in the stories included in the present volume. The title story
eveals the author's concern for the marginal, the transgressive and the
ictimised woman.

Hyder's early stories and novels established her as an innovator in
nguage and form; she was credited with the introduction of modernist
chniques and sensibility into Urdu fiction. Her epic *Aag ka Darya* (The
iver of Fire) occupies a place in the South Asian canon analagous to that
Gabriel Garcia Marquez's (q.v.) *One Hundred Years of Solitude* (1967) in
e Western canon. However, the novel preceded Garcia Marquez's
asterwork by a decade, and Hyder disclaims all knowledge of magic
ealism. She questions the boundaries between long and short fiction,
ressing that her stories often cover the timespan of novels."

—*Aamer Hussein*
Contemporary World Writers
(St. James Press, published in the U.K.)

STERLING SERIES ON SHORT STORIES

1. **BETWEEN TEARS & LAUGHTER**
   Short Stories
   Mulk Raj Anand

2. **PADMAVATI, THE HARLOT AND OTHER STORIES**
   Kamala Das

3. **THE WOMAN AND OTHER STORIES**
   Gangadhar Gadgil

4. **CONTEMPORARY URDU SHORT STORIES:**
   AN ANTHOLOGY
   Jai Ratan (Ed.)

5. **MIDDLING TALES**
   Gemma M. D'Cunha

6. ***MANSHA YAD'S TAMASHA* & OTHER STORIES**
   Jamil Azar (Ed.)

7. **SPICED LAUGHTER**
   A Collection of Humorous Short Stories
   Dalip Singh

8. **REFLECTIONS TWENTY-ONE INDIAN**
   SHORT STORIES
   Roman Basu (Ed.)

9. **LANGUAGE OF LOVE: AN ANTHOLOGY OF**
   SHORT STORIES
   Aruna Jethwani (Ed.)

10. **THE MUSIC MAN AND OTHER STORIES**
    Vijay Shankar

11. **BEST LOVED FOLK TALES OF INDIA**
    P.C. Roy Chaudhury (Ed.)

Published by
Sterling Publishers Pvt. Ltd.

THE
STREET SINGERS
OF LUCKNOW
AND OTHER STORIES

Qurratulain Hyder

A Sterling Paperback

STERLING PAPERBACKS
AN IMPRINT OF
Sterling Publishers (P) Ltd
L-10, Green Park Extension, New Delhi-110016

The Street Singers of Lucknow and Other Stories
©1996 Qurratulain Hyder
ISBN 81 207 1851 8

Published by Sterling Publishers Pvt. Ltd.,New Delhi.
Laserset by L.C. Publishing Service, New Delhi.
Printed at Ramprintograph. Delhi - 51
The painting on the cover is by Qurratulain Hyder

Contents

Contents

1
The Street Singers of Lucknow

I

Bhooray Qawwal and Party clapped their hands in vigorous rhythm as they sang of the Lord Prophet's Mystical Night Journey to the Celestial Spheres. The Lord Prophet rides a resplendent, winged stallion. In an instant, he reaches the Holy City of Jerusalem—he ascends from the grey-blue Rock and traverses the Seven Heavens, meeting the earlier prophets on the Way of Light. In an instant, he reaches the Presence of God. When he returns to earth the chain of his door is still swinging. The mystical experience of the human soul. The Profound Mystery.

Bhooray Khan paused for effect and surveyed his audience. A petromax shed its fading light on the courtyard of Peer Handey Shah's tomb. One of the devotees reverently placed a lantern in front of the singers. It was long past midnight. The shrine's peacocks had already perched themselves on the branches of the overhanging bunyan. Some of them walked majestically along the parapet of the whitewashed mausoleum.

Bhooray Khan and his emaciated choir, his rural audience, the sleepy peacocks, they were all part of the Great Mystery. So was the medieval shrine surrounded by dark mango trees. It was a fairly unknown saint's shrine. Nobody knew his real name. He was merely called Peer Handey Shah, Saint of the Gas Lamp, after the petromax somebody had donated to the tomb long ago. Perhaps the peer never existed. Whatever is happening, is perhaps not real. Or, what is the basis or substance of it all? If Peer Handey Shah is non-existent, what is, that exists? And if this is not the only reality which surrounds us, what is, that lies beyond? Besides, like many artists, writers, and poets, some saints are lucky that the world knows them. Some have only a few devotees to light lamps at their graves. Some have none at all.

Maybe this was the shrine some unknown German travellers had sketched when they passed by on horseback. And its woodcut was printed, with heavy Gothic lettering, in a heavy Gothic folio, in some faraway German town—four hundred years ago. Who were those passers-by, and how did they come to the remote forests of India? And why did everything happen which happened, earlier and afterwards?

In an instant he reaches the Celestial Spheres, in an instant he returns. . . .

Bhooray Khan, the fabulous singer, and Nabban Khan, his expert tabla-player—why didn't they become rich and famous, while many others like them did? The Profound Mystery.

- The devout who visited Peer Handey Shah's dargah were mostly oil-pressers, weavers, potters, butchers, peasants and their womenfolk, who spent their lives in flat-roofed hovels and were buried in mud graves. They were supposedly the beloved of God. Like the old woman Sharifan—destitute widow who was saying her Isha prayer in a corner of the shrine. *I begin with the Name of God. I recite the Credo of Mohammed. There is no god but God. And Mohammed is His Prophet. Lead us on the Straight Path. Thine is the glory. I begin with the Name of God. From Thee we come and to Thee we return. When the sky is rent asunder, when the stars scatter and the oceans roll together, when the graves are hurled about, each soul shall know what it has done and what it has failed to do. . . . I seek refuge in the Lord of Daybreak from the mischief of His creation, from the mischief of the night when she spreads her darkness. By the light of the day. Your Lord has not forsaken you . . . .* She went through the ritual movements and kept repeating a few jumbled-up verses of the *Quran*, for she did not know how to properly say her ritual prayers. All her life, whenever she could get some respite from her backbreaking labour, she communed with God in the same haphazard manner. Her only daughter had been axed to death by her in-laws. They had bribed the police and got away. Sharifan went from house to house doing odd jobs and earned a few annas a day. Technically, she should be among the first to enter the gates of Paradise.

And the humble, unknown qawwal, his aged half-blind tabla-player, and his fellow-singers, and the lowly people who listened to them rapturously, and the poor traders who were selling their modest ware in the Urs fair—they were all duly informed from time to time that they were to inherit the Kingdom of God.

Outside the shrine, rows of thin, dark men in tattered sarongs, and women in patched, tight pyjamas sat on their haunches, selling sweets and peanuts and cones of peeled sugarcane. Tiny kerosene lamps burnt at each "stall". A venerable old man with a white goatee was hawking his Japanese trinkets. "Four annas for everything—four annas—four annas—" His entire stock consisted of a few hairpins, tinsel earrings, glass beads and plastic bangles.

"How much for this clip, uncle?" an attractive, dusky girl of fourteen asked eagerly.

"Everything four annas, Bitiya."

The girl adjusted her torn dupatta of pink Japanese georgette and knelt down on the grass to have a better look at the treasure-trove. She wore parrot-green shalwar-kameez of "banana" silk, and worn-out, dusty tennis shoes. After some deliberation she untied a corner of her stole and took out her savings. She looked at the solitary eight-anna bit dejectedly, because she wanted to buy a present for her younger sister too. "All right, Uncle, give us those clips—the pink one," she said thoughtfully.

The old man handed her a pair of plastic clasps shaped like butterflies. The girl's face lighted up as she touched them lovingly.

"Rashke Qamar—O Rashke Qamar, have you dropped dead?" A woman called out from somewhere. The girl paid the shopkeeper and started running towards the saint's tomb.

In the forecourt of the dargah, Bhooray Khan Qawwal had made his final bows, collected his tips and made way for the one-eyed jester and his party. The clown had taken his seat behind a small, portable harmonium. He was dressed in a discoloured sleeping suit and embroidered waistcoat of purple velvet. A fez sat jauntily on his head. A consumptive woman of about forty sat next to him. The night had become chilly and a cold wind blew among the mangoes. The delicate-looking woman wrapped herself in a rough shawl and dragged a small drum in front of her.

A girl of seven was sitting beside her. The child had big, round eyes, full of wonder. She was looking intently at the motley audience. The woman boxed her ears and hissed: "Bloody mongrel. Sing. Come near the harmonium."

"Pick me up, please, Auntie," the child replied gently.

"Bleeding bastard. We starve for days on end. We have become all skin and bones. But this illegitimate daughter of Rustam Pehelwan is getting fatter by the day. How can I lift you, you fat lump of corruption?"

The girl in green, called Rashke Qamar, Enoy of the Moon, reached the dais panting. The child looked up and gave her a beatific smile. "Bajia," she exclaimed happily and spread her thin little arms towards the girl. Rashke Qamar helped her sit near the harmonium. Carefully the child tried to cover her deformed leg under her skirted pyjamas. The one-eyed joker bent down his head over the keyboard and started playing a sad, haunting tune. The woman played the drum. The older girl placed her right hand over her ear and began singing an Urdu ghazal. The child accompanied her in a small, sweet voice:

The journey is tough, how long would ye sleep?
Destination is hard to reach.
Nasim! arise, and tie your sash, roll up your mat.
Get ready to leave, the night is short.

The audience understood. They nodded approvingly. They had been perfectly attuned to Bhooray Khan as well. The older girl in green sang with greater fervour:

Youth and charm, pomp, and wealth,
Are matters all of numbered breaths. . .
Extinction awaits with folded hands,
Moment by moment the warning comes
To pack up and leave, saddle and go.
Like the empty palms of a beggar am I,
Bereft of all desire.
Attached to detachment, my heart reflects
My True Love's Radiant Face.

"Allah is Truth. . . Allah is Truth. . . Allah. . ." a jet-black, half-naked, "God-intoxicated" fakir screeched in his reedy voice and began rolling on the courtyard floor. "There is naught but Allah . . . Naught but Allah. . . Naught but Allagh. . ."

Life follows not a steady course,
Grief comes after transitory joy . . .
The girls continued.

A cousin of the village landlord, who had lost his property in family litigation, pounded the floor with his fists. He wept and repeated: *"Grief comes after transitory joy. . . . Grief comes. . .Grief. . . .* O beneficient merciful Allah. . . I have seen Thy mercy . . . ha . . . ha . . . ho . . . ho . . . ho . . ."

Hold your tongue, don't rant and rave,
The ecstasy can drive one mad . . .
The girl in green addressed the ruined zamindar as she sang out the next couplet of the mystical ghazal.

By now many people had begun to swoon in a kind of spiritual delirium. Some rose to their feet and started whirling in the centre of the quadrangle. A few shouted: "Allah is Truth . . . Nothing exists but God." The "dancing dervishes" began to whirl ecstatically. All this was part of the deep response to a god, effective mystical ghazal or qawwali. Bhooray Khan had evoked identical audience participation in Sufi music.

Now the crowd was working itself into a spiritual frenzy. The one-eyed man picked up the lame child and placed her on his left shoulder. She sat there like a monkey, clapped her tiny hands with all her strength and continued to sing with her sister. The ghazal reached its crescendo and came to an end in a shower of descending notes. The audience began to throw two-anna bits at the consumptive woman who eagerly gathered them in her shawl.

"Give us a pice. . . Give us a pice. . .Give us. . ." Rashke Qamar chanted as she went dancing towards the poverty-stricken devotees. In all she collected seven rupees and twelve annas. She looked at the coins disappointedly and tied them in a corner of her stole.

The crowd broke up. The family got down from the dais. The elderly woman turned towards the saint's flower-laden grave and muttered the Benediction. The anniversary of the Sufi's death, or Urs anniversary of the "Union" of a saint's soul with the Supreme Spirit was over.

Outside, in a thatched shed which served as an inn, the *nanbai* was busy packing up. It was the last evening of Peer Handey Shah's fair. The singers had left their belongings in a corner of the make-shift restaurant. As they entered the shed, Rashke Qamar went behind the oven and opened a small tin trunk. Carefully, she put in the packet of pink plastic clips and locked it again. She was weeping silently.

"Don't you start snivelling again, you luckless clot!" the aunt hissed again.

"Do eat something before you go," the hotel-keeper said kindly. He served delicious meat curry and flat, crisp bread to the pitiful band of itinerant musicians. The grotesque clown, the sharp-tongued matron and the two melancholy girls sat down on the mud floor and began eating ravenously and in grim silence.

The portly *nanbai* gave them water to drink in bronze Moradabadi cups. They licked their fingers. The half-blind man belched and uttered a loud *Praise be to the Beneficient Lord.* The family thanked the *nanbai* profusely. He didn't charge them for the food. The clown tied the portable harmonium to his waist and placed his bedroll and trunk on his head with the deftness of a railway coolie. The woman picked up the drum. Jamila, the lame child, perched herself on the shoulder of her elder sister. They said *Allah be with you* to the chop-house-owner and came out. As they crossed the fair grounds, little Jamila turned her head and cast longing eyes at the booths of clay dolls and glass bangles. The jester heaved a deep sigh. He looked up at the white-washed dome of the dargah and whined aloud: "Ho . . . ho . . . Wah. . . Peer Handey Shah. . . We had come to your holy durbar with high hopes. And what did you give us? Rupees nine, annas six and pies eight only. *Allah is Great.*"

"Furqan Manzil," Lucknow.

II

The wheezy old Deputy Saheb sat in the back verandah dyeing his hair. His wife, known as "Diptiayin"—Deputy's Lady—stood in front, dutifully holding the hand-mirror. "Dipti Saheb" was tunelessly humming an ante-deluvian ghazal. He seemed very pleased with himself as he started trimming his moustaches. All of a sudden, he raised his head and said, "Wife, shall I marry this wench—what's her name—Rashke Qamar? Strictly on a temporary basis, you know, and with your permission, of course. . ."

Diptiayin banged the mirror on the marble-top table, and waddled off towards her room, dragging her gold-embroidered Mushal-style slippers. Her lord and master left his moustache undone, picked up his glasses and got up. A little sheepishly he sauntered away towards the outer apartments, where the men of the house spent most of their time.

Diptiayin returned to the verandah and yelled, "Chhedoo's wife, send for Qamrun's aunt at once."

Chhedoo's wife emerged from the basement and trundled down to the gatehouse.

"Furqan Manzil" had been built in the style of early 19th century "Lucknow rococo" by Deputy Saheb's great-grandfather. He was supposed to have been the governor of Qandhar before he came down to the Kingdom of Oudh. But Deputy Saheb's enemies maintained that the said ancestor was in fact a groom in the stables of King Wajid Ali Shah. Allah knows best.

The present descendant was a retired deputy collector of the provincial civil service. His wife was well known for her meanness. She had let out the basement rooms of the sprawling *haveli* to a lot of poor families. They paid her the rent and their women and children worked as unpaid drudges in Furqan Manzil. At daybreak the men went out to work as kite-makers, and barrow-boys or loafed about in the labyrinth of alleyways which surrounded the mansion. Furqan Manzil's gatehouse also contained a number of down-and-out tenants. One of the dingy, lightless rooms was occupied by young Rashke Qamar

alias Qamrun, her one-eyed uncle, her crazy aunt Hurmuzi
and her lame sister Jamila. God, what a family!. . .

Chhedoo's wife was greeted by the one-eyed uncle
who sat in the doorway, arduously shaving the head of the
local mullah. Inside, in the smoke-filled room, Aunt
Hurmuzi was busy fanning a brazier. As usual, the poor,
disabled Jamila was lying on her cot, brooding. Chhedoo's
wife lifted the jute curtain and hollered: "O Qamrun's
aunt. Diptiayin wishes to have a word with you. At once."

"Shoo...shoo...Azrael's courier. . .get lost. . .scram. . ."
Qamrun's aunt roared back and hurled a pair of tongs at
the visitor.

After a while Hurmuzi Begum entered the vast
courtyard, shuffling her feet. Diptiayin was waiting for her
in the verandah. Hurmuzi Begum went up to her, growling.

"Sit down." The lady of the house pointed towards the
tiled floor.

She sat down.

"Qamrun's aunt," Diptiayin began imperiously, "I had
taken you in as a tenant, thinking you to be a God-fearing
honest woman."

"So, ain't I a God-fearing, honest woman?"

"I took pity on your crippled niece."

"Oh, thanks."

"You told me your husband was a barber."

"So? Do you think he is a grass-cutter?"

"People said to me that you all were street-singers, no-
good gypsies, who went begging from door to door. . ."

"We didn't come a-begging at your door, lady."

Diptiayin was enraged. But the old woman was known
to be cranky, and that was the way she talked.

"Hold your tongue, Hurmuzi, or I'll beat you with my
own shoes. People were right when they said that you all
were low-down *khangies*, veiled courtesans, of
Hussainabad. I didn't believe them. Because the Lord
Prophet has said: *Never suspect any one until you have
seen with your own eyes*. Well, the other evening I did see
your dear niece slipping out, covered in her white burqa.
At that time, after sun-down, was she going out to hear a
religious sermon? She will come to no good. The slut. I'm
afraid I can't allow you to stay here any longer, Qamrun's
aunt."

Agha Safdar Hussain "Farhad" Qandhari—student of M.A. (Persian) at the University of Lucknow, a budding Urdu poet and Deputy Saheb's only son and heir, had got up at 10 o'clock that Sunday morning. He had just finished his tea in his luxurious, airy bedroom on the first floor, when he heard his mother quarrelling, as usual, with one of her miserable tenants. He jumped out of his fourposter and came downstairs. In the verandah he found Rashke Qamar's foul-mouthed aunt confronting his formidable mother. He yawned and asked in a bored voice: "Ammie Jan, is it about that girl again?"

"Son," Diptiayin complained melodramatically, "you know how good I have been to these ungrateful worms. They were homeless. I gave them shelter. They were penniless. I loaned full twenty rupees to that one-eyed fool to set up a shop as a barber. I sent Rashke Qamar to school. I taught her manners. And this is how they repay me."

"Ammie Jan," Agha Farhad cut in impatiently, "leave the matter to me. I'll take care of it." He turned to the woman: "Qamrun's aunt, you may go."

She got up groaning and trotted off.

Lately, Farhad had sensed his old father's lecherous interest in the tenants' pretty niece. Red with anger and shame, he marched down to the courtyard where, under a flowering magnolia, the girl in question sat by the water-tap washing her face with Pear's soap. Farhad cast a glance at her sea-green stole of fine muslin and her glittering Hyderabadi bangles. Her long hair reeked of perfumed oil. If they are so poor how does she afford such luxuries? Tart.

Rashke Qamar looked up. Farhad saw her lovely face and his anger vanished. He said amiably: "Qamrun, please come upstairs to my room."

"Upstairs to your room?" she giggled. "After all this hoo-ha?"

Slut. Farhad flushed a deep crimson. "Qamrun, I wish you well." He said gravely, "I would like to talk to you and try to help you out of this. . . this sordid mess."

The girl noticed the young master's seriousness and answered soberly: "Yes, sir. I'll be there in a few minutes."

Upstairs in his bedroom Agha Farhad reclined on a chaise-lounge under a stain-glass window, a picture of aristocratic, Old World elegance and well-being. He was absently leafing through an anthology of classical Urdu poetry. A cool, refreshing breeze was blowing into the room. It was a mild, pleasant winter morning.

"May I come in, sir?" the girl asked, parting the velvet curtains.

"Yes, do," Farhad got up and put the heavy volume on a rosewood tallboy. He returned to the chaise-lounge, saying a trifle nervously: "Let me come straight to the point. You all came here exactly two years ago, didn't you? As long you went to school there was peace. Now there is always some trouble because of you. Why did you leave school?"

"Ah, some blue-blooded young ladies didn't want to sit next to me in the classroom. I said what the hell. Myself don't like to mix with snooty females. I have my self-respect, you know. So I stopped going to that august centre of learning."

"Sit down, Rashke Qamar."

She squatted down on the Bokhara carpet.

"Now," Farhad said expansively, regaining his composure, "you must tell me all about yourself. Why this aura of mystery around you?"

"Mystery?"

"Your secret life, shall we say."

"Only the rich and the powerful have mysteries and secret lives, Mian. We the riff-raff have nothing to hide."

"Come, come," Farhad said uncomfortably. "You know, busybodies keep telling Mother all manner of nonsense about you. It upsets her."

"What they say is perfectly true, sir."

"Eh . . .?"

"Yes, sir. Perhaps that's the only good point I have. I am truthful. Never tell lies."

"Look, when you came here and your uncle wished to hire a room in our gatehouse, he said business was not good in the countryside and he had come to try his luck in the city."

"What he said was also true, Mian. We sang and clowned at country fairs. There was very little money in it.

And we got dog-tired trudging from village to village earning a pittance for our performances. So my Aunt Hurmuzi said, let's go back to town where we belong. When we returned to Lucknow someone told us there was a room vacant in your outhouse. So we moved in and gave up our old trade. People out here don't need us to entertain them. They have their radio sets, and the cinema. Uncle Jumman became a barber. What's so mysterious about it?"

"What do you intend doing now, Rashke Qamar?" Farhad asked after a pause. "Don't you want to get married?"

"Get married?"

"Don't girls marry when they grow up?"

"Mian, you must be naive. Even high-born young ladies find it difficult to get suitable husbands these days. Who the hell would marry a street-singer? Forget it, Mian. Show me this book you were reading."

She went to the tallboy and picked up the anthology. Farhad watched her languorous, alluring gait. She leaned against the chest-of-drawers, opened the book, and began humming a ghazal.

"A little louder!"

"Hush—! Close the doors. Diptiayin may hear!" She selected a ghazal of Mir Taqi Mir and started reciting it tunefully. When she had finished, he jumped up with boyish enthusiasm. "Shake hands, Rashke Qamar," he said, "I have hit upon your future career. I'll groom you as a poetess."

"A poetess? For goodness' sake, Mian, I can sing a ghazal. Can't write one."

"I can. In fact, according to many people, I am quite talented. . ." he added modestly. "I'll ghost-write ghazals for you and get you invited to all the best poetic symposia—mushairas—Wow! With that voice and style of yours you will be a smashing hit in no time. I know my *mushaira* audiences. . . ."

III

"This is All India Radio, Lucknow. The All India Ladies Mushaira is being relayed from the Silver Pavilion, Qaiser Bagh. You have just listened to the poems of Miss Nazneen

Barelvi. Now the promising young poetess of Lucknow, Miss Rashke Qamar, will recite her latest ghazals. . ."

After the poetic symposium was over, the promising young poetess hurriedly put on her veil and slipped out of the gilded hall where once operas were staged for the Kings of Oudh. Farhad was waiting for the girl in a corridor.

"Well done, my Rose of Shiraz," he said effusively.

Rashke Qamar wrapped herself properly in her new burqa of shimmering black Lady Hamilton. They hastened out of the Silver Pavilion.

"I hope nosey females didn't pester you with unnecessary questions," he said anxiously as they got into a victoria.

"Questions are always unnecessary. Where are we going now?"

He grinned. "I am taking you to meet a very dear friend of mine. He, too, has some ideas about you in his fertile brain. Let's first pick up Jamila. Pata Nala—" he told the coachman.

IV

A jute curtain hung over the main door of a modest house in Pata Nala. Inside, in the courtyard, a well-dressed Jamila sat on a cane-stool, knitting. A chicken coop stood under a leafy guava tree. Hurmuzi Begum was busy in the kitchen. Uncle Jumman had gone out to work—as a bookbinder's assistant. A thoroughly respectable, peaceful lower middle-class household. "It's a crystal palace compared to the cubbyhole in which we lived in the gatehouse of Furqan Manzil!" Aunt Hurmuzi had exclaimed when they had moved in a few months ago.

"Now that we have gone up a bit on the social ladder, shouldn't I join a high-class hair-cutting saloon in Hazrat Gunj and call myself a hair-stylist?" Uncle Jumman had asked, chuckling.

"Yes, indeed, and cut our noses along with your customers' hair. Let the world know that the celebrated Miss Rashke Qamar Lucknawi's uncle is a barber. Our Qamrun is making enough money from her radio and her *mushairas*. And the good Lord has sent Farhad Mian to her as a protector-angel. So why must you work?"

"Because," her husband had retorted indignantly, "I would not like to be called Qamrun's tout."

"Ask your Angel of Mercy to get Uncle a job as a shop assistant or something," the lame, surly Jamila had suggested sarcastically.

The victoria stopped in front of Rashke Qamar's house. "They have come," Hurmuzi Khanum remarked happily, peering out of the kitchen window. Farhad and Qamrun entered the courtyard. "Come along," Farhad said to Jamilun breezily. "We are going to a very special place called Thinker's Den."

V

NARENDRA KUMAR VERMA
M.A. (Gold Medalist)
Writer, Journalist and Art Adviser

"Even his name-plate is arty-crafty!" Farhad winked as he escorted the girls into the gallery. The board with florid lettering was half covered by a money-plant. The luxuriant creeper sprouted out of a VAT 69. The bottle was placed upon a tiny rock surrounded by multi-coloured pebbles. Overhead, an alcove displayed a portrait of Tagore who somehow looked like God the Father.

A Dancing Shiva peeped through the doorway.

Inside, the spacious sitting-room was cluttered with more South Indian bronzes, Assamese folk designs, and a lot of studio pottery. The walls were adorned with Noh and Kathakali masks and Jamini Roys. A sitar stood under a picture of Mirza Ghalib. The shelves overflowed with books on Modern Theatre, Modern Art and New Wave Cinema. Trendy Urdu magazines from Pakistan lay scattered on a Tibetan rug. The girls looked bewildered. Farhad beamed. An agile young man with fuzzy hair and horn-rimmed glasses darted in from somewhere. He was impeccably dressed in a *kurta* of handloom silk, a Nehru jacket and white *churidar* pyjamas. He looked good-hearted and genial and grinned widely as he welcomed the guests.

It was a bachelor's apartment. He called out to the "*chhokra* boy" to get some tea. When the servant didn't appear, he picked up the boat-shaped teapot and made a dash for the kitchen.

A pale, thin girl came in. As she sat down nervously on the edge of a divan, Rashke Qamar whispered to Farhad, "You haven't yet told me about the host. Who is he?"

"Oh, he?" Farhad answered airily. "Capital fellow. Childhood friend of mine. Only son of wealthy parents. They live in their ancestral *haveli* at Narahi. He devotes his time and energy to the selfless service of art and culture, here in this flat. The building belongs to his Pop. I had told him about you. He promptly chalked out a scheme for the promotion of your career. He'll tell you about it himself."

Verma returned with the teapot, flopped down on the yellow Mirzapuri carpet and smiled benignly.

Jamila was talking to the frightened-looking girl in the far end of the room. Farhad whispered to the host, "And pray, who may she be?"

"Oh, she—?"

"Yeh. Big game from the hills?"

"This Greek-nosed, lotus-eyed beauty with no waist looks like a chick from the hills? You need a pair of glasses . . . Moti . . . come here. Time you learnt how to pour tea. Miss Rashke Qamar, I would request you to kindly train my protege in the art of gracious living."

"*Leave your rustic kitchen, my Sarwan, take up the forks and knives. Shed your peasant skirt, my Sarwan, put on English gowns. . .*" Farhad sang out mirthfully.

"What's that—?" Verma asked, intrigued.

"An old folk song of Delhi. Long before the Mutiny of 1857, the English Resident of Delhi had fallen in love with a Jat lass of Haryana. So the people made up a song about William Frazer and Sarwan."

"What happened to them?" asked Verma.

"William Frazer was done in. In some other case. I don't know what became of poor Sarwan."

"If some Feranghee falls in love with my Sarwan here," Verma declared with a flourish, "I, too, shall do him in."

"Wouldn't you introduce the young lady to us?" asked Farhad. "Where did you discover her?"

"Last week," Verma explained smoothly, "I had accompanied my mother to the fair of Ali Gunj. Ma often

visits the Hanuman temple over there and prays fervently
to the monkey god that I mend my ways and get married.
It so happened that day that as Mother went into the
temple yours truly sallied forth, taking photographs for a
pictorial feature. It was then that God in His infinite
Wisdom directed my steps to the tamarind tree under
which this myna, this bulbul, stood warbling woodland
notes."

"Speak in prose," Farhad said.

"This is Motibai, a talented *patar*, a rural courtesan, of
Faizabad district. A koel straight from the sylvan glades of
Ayodhya. Exponent of Oudh's folk songs."

"And if your mother comes to know of this nightingale
now residing in the rose-garden of your heart—?"

"Right now Ma hasn't the foggiest; may come to know
soon. But what can I do? It seems to be Lord Hanuman's
will. After all I found the nymph in the compound of his
temple, didn't I? Now, listen. I'm going to start a Songbirds'
Club. These three young ladies will be its chief warblers.
We'll give concerts in the city, tour the land, broadcast
over AIR, and so forth. The Songbirds would be a fly-away
hit. Here is the motif I've thought up for our letterhead."
He pulled out a drawing from underneath a terracotta
horse. A damsel with elongated eyes languidly tuned the
tamboura under a sprawling mango. Tiny birds sat on the
tree's branches. Farhad looked at the decorative sketch
and passed it on to Rashke Qamar.

"Moti——Moti——" Verma called the girl as though
she were the house cat or a caged parrot. "Moti——say
Sadaf."

"Sadaph . . ."

"Sadaf with an F. . ."

"Sadaf with an eph. . ."

"Good God! All right. Say Sadaf Ara Begum."

"Sadaph Ara Begum."

"Moti still speaks her village dialect. From tomorrow
I'll start teaching her correct Urdu. Now, Moti, I have told
you what *sadaf* means."

"Yes, Sarkar. Pearl."

"Don't you go on Sarkaring me. Yes. Pearl. Fine. Moti
in Hindi-Urdu. Sadaf in Persian. What is *Sadaf Ara Begum*?
Your new professional name! Elegant and Mughal. Suites

your delicate sharp features and milky-white complexion."
He turned to Jamila who had all this while been listening
carefully to this rather bizzare conversation.

He looked at her intently for a few seconds and
exclaimed, "Kumari Jalabala Lehri. . . !"

"I beg your pardon?" Jamila asked, stared.

"Your new professional name. You look like a sensitive,
dreamy-eyed Bengali sylph. Lyrical and Tagorean. Kumari
Jolbala Lahiri. Water-Maiden from the Land of Rivers.
You've just arrived from Calcutta to join the Songbirds
Club. You learnt your music in Santiniketan and sat at
the holy feet of Gurudev Tagore."

"Listen, Verma Saheb," Jamila answered patiently, and
in measured tones, "My name is Jamil-un-Nissa Begum
and I have arrived from Pata Nala. I learnt my music
nowhere and I sat at nobody's holy feet."

"My good woman, I'm only trying to make your career
for you."

"Career—what's that?"

"Your professional life. Your future."

"When God Almighty could not make my career for me,
how would you, sir?"

"Kumari Jolbala Lahiri—Daughter of the Waves," Verma
replied firmly.

"Why Lahiri—? Because I waver and wobble?" Jamila
asked, looking ruefully at her shrivelled leg.

"For heaven's sake, Farhad, explain to this crazy girl
that Lahiri is a lovely Bengali surname."

"Verma Saheb, my sister is a bit touchy about her
physical handicap. But I'll bring her round. Tell me, when
do we start the rehearsals?" Rashke Qamar asked briskly,
already a hardened professional.

Verma beamed at her and started writing:

SONGBIRDS CLUB, LUCKNOW.
Chief Artistes
Sadaf Ara Begum
Miss Rashke Qamar Lucknawi
Kumari Jalbala Lahiri

Looking very pleased with himself he said, "Pity I can't
improve upon Rashke Qamar—Envy of the Moon."

VI

"Hello . . . Hello . . . Yes this is Verma speaking. Oh, hello, Adab Arz . . . How are you? Long time no see . . . Ah, so you were away in Delhi. Well, you did miss our premier concert. Oh, yes, it was a thundering success. An honourable minister inaugurated the Songbirds Club. There were impassioned speeches on our Glorious Cultural Heritage. We launched our girlies—er—our talented artistes in the full glare of publicity . . .Yes. House Full. Thanks. Nice of you to say that. Of course I depend on your encouragement. Pardon . . . ? No. Our songstresses specialise in Light Music. You know—Ghazal. Thumri. Dadra. Kajri. Geet. Etcetra. Yes. Rave reviews . . . Right now? Well—er—I am sorry, it's Tuesday evening. I have to take my mother to the temple for *keertan.* I'm going to Narahi right away. Thanks a lot. I do need your good wishes, bye . . ."

Narendra Kumar Verma put down the receiver and returned to the Ottoman, saying, "Mothers are always such a help."

"Liar." Agha Farhad grinned. 'I am taking my mother to the temple.' Who was it?"

"Distant-ooq. Threatened to come over to personally congratulate me on the success of the concert."

"Distant-ooq? Oh, that Farooq-pain-in-the-neck-Qureshi?"

"Yeh. And where is my blue Angora?"

"Purring in the kitchen," Farhad replied.

"My skylark has cooked a sumptuous dinner for you tonight."

"Your metaphors are getting a bit mixed up."

"My magpie has made a pie . . ."

Rashke Qamar looked at them: They are schoolboys treating us as their newest toy trains. "Why must you always be so flippant about poor Sadaf?" she said to Verma sharply. "She is a good girl."

"All three of you are good girls," he gushed. "Look, I have thought of another scheme for the furtherance of your literary career."

"So help me God."

"Listen. I am going to publish an Urdu magazine. It shall be called *Gohar-i-Shab-Charagh*—the pearl that lights up the night." He winked at Farhad.

"That's a gem of a name. You are priceless, Verma. Sadaf Ara Begum and Gohar-i-Shab-Charagh—Fantastic!" Farhad said approvingly.

"And in the very first issue I shall do a write-up on our poetess here. I have some possible titles in mind." Quickly he scribbled a few lines on a piece of paper and read out:

"One: Rashke Qamar's Poetry —Its Lyrical Existentialism. Two: The Influence of Mallarme on Rashke Qamar."

"Who is Mallarme?" Farhad interrupted.

"Never mind. Three: Image and Idea in Rashke Qamar's Longer Poems. Four: A New Voice in Modern Urdu Ghazal. Five: Rashke Qamar's Views on Art, or, Her Philosophy of Life. Six: The Profound Significance of the Succession of Days and Nights in Rashke Qamari's Time Scheme."

"I liked the last title," Farhad remarked with a glint in his eye.

"Aren't you two ashamed of yourselves, making fun of me?" Rashke Qamar asked with deep sadness.

"Ma'm. I'm doing top-class public relations work for you," Verma replied solemnly.

Jamila tried to get up with the help of her crutches. Both young men rushed to her aid. Suddenly Jamila bent down her head and started crying.

"Jamila. . . Jamila . . . child. . . what happened? Are you all right?" Verma asked with genuine concern. Farhad offered her a cup of coffee.

In a few minutes she calmed down and wiped her tears. Sadaf came running from the kitchen.

"What happened, Jamila?" Verma repeated.

"Sorry, I have become so weepy," she said. "We have known nothing but hardships and humiliations, and all of a sudden our way of life has become so different. It makes me scared. It's too good to be true."

"Don't be absurd, Jamila," Verma said with sincerity.

"My sister, here, is a bit of an oddball," Rashke Qamar said apologetically. "Shsh . . . Jamilun, stop it. I feel so ashamed."

The young girl stared at her older sister and said with sudden defiance. "Your Almighty God was not ashamed of making such a sorry mess of our lives. Why should I be ashamed? But you watch out!"

Farhad coloured and looked away. Verma fidgeted with the spoons. He offered her another cup of coffee.

"Thanks," she aid coolly. They were looking at her expectantly and in a kind of nameless fear. In an instant she had become their Conscience, crippled and unused.

"And I dare you to publish our true background in your *Gohar-i-Shab-Charagh*, instead of this ludicrous nonsense you are planning to make up about my sister, even if it is meant to be joke."

"I'm sorry, Jamila, I mean well," Verma said, crestfallen. "Please understand, we are your well-wishers. And we certainly don't make fun of you."

Jamila was gazing at her twisted right leg. "Some lives get twisted and useless like this poor limb of mine," she said slowly. "Nobody's fault. What is the great mystery behind it all? My mother conked off a few minutes after my birth. I entered the world with this ghastly deformity. My Aunt Hurmuzi dragged me up on a diet of abuses. I crawled about in the filthy back-lanes of our neighbourhood and played in the gutters. Guttersnipe. That's what I was. All of us were . . .and still are. Only the way of addressing us has changed. Surely you know who we are, don't you?"

Verma and Farhad looked acutely embarrassed. They belonged to an over-ripe civilisation of the Nawabs in which a lot of things were left politely unsaid. This girl seemed to be a barbarian who had turned up from the backwoods of life to disturb their tranquil, cultured lives. Now she seemed to be enjoying her benefactors' discomfiture as she continued, "Aunt Hurmuzi contacted T.B. Most of her savings were spent on medical treatment. The doctor advised her to go the sanatorium at Bhawali. And there we were, all alone in the world and not a soul to look after us."

"What about your Uncle Jumman?" Verma asked.

"Jumman Khan," the girl replied, "was a lone, funny-looking barber. He had first come to our house to shave my head, in accordance with some religious custom, when I was six days old. He grew fond of me and began visiting us frequently. As I grew older he took me to the bazaar and bought me peanuts. We had very little laughter in our lives. He clowned and made even Aunt Hurmuzi laugh. Because of her illness she had lost her patrons. We could not afford a servant. Jumman Khan often helped out. My aunt treated him as a menial. He was so humble, he didn't mind. He was a childless widower and craved for a little kindness from fellow human, just as we did. He offered to accompany us to Bhawali.

"Jumman Khan had quite a few bad habits. He ate opium when he was not gambling. And he never missed a cock-fight when he had a few annas left in his pocket. He was a lovable, warm-hearted rascal and my sister and I doted on him.

"He was also very pious and honest. As he escorted us to the hill-station, my aunt gave him all the money she had, for safe-keeping.

"When the train reached Kathgodam, we got down from the ladies third-class compartment and looked about. There was no Jumman Khan. The ground slipped from under our feet. We looked around frantically and found him in a corner of the platform howling away for all he was worth. 'Somebody picked my pocket while I was fast asleep,' he muttered between his sobs, 'Skin me alive. Behead me. Throw me to the leopards.'

"It seemed the end of the world for us. My aunt threw a fit. 'You half-blind toad. You offspring of a two-pice whore! You pig-eating scavenger!' My aunt's abuses where always quite original and colourful. 'You mother-selling pimp!' she went on in her fury. 'You have gone and lost my life's savings playing cards with some fellow-passenger and you tail-less pie-dog, you have the cheek to tell me that you were robbed!'

"Jumman Khan stood petrified. A crowd collected around us. I clung to him and began to cry. Somehow, with the clarity of a child's mind I had sensed that he was telling the truth. Suddenly he clutched the miniature *Quran* he wore in a silver locket round his neck, and declaimed: 'As God and the Lord Prophet are my witness, I am telling the truth. I swear by the Holy Book. I swear by the Holy Five! . . . .'

---

1. Mohammed, Ali, Fatima, Hasan, Hussain.

"My aunt is a deeply religious woman. She stared hard at him as he whimpered, and believed him. We accepted the disaster as part of our general misfortune and sat down at the end of the platform. Homeless paupers. Wistfully we watched the motor cars and buses leaving one by one for the mountain road. There lay Bhawali, Nainital, Almora, Ranikhet, on the misty, pine-covered peaks of the Himalayas. The foothills loomed right in front of us like an insurmountable wall. Bhawali was now beyond our reach.

"Luckily, Jumman Khan had brought his barber's kit along. He began shaving the third-class passengers who arrived from the plains. Bajia and I could sing. So the moment a train arrived at the terminus, we rushed towards the first and second class compartments and sang with all our vocal strength. Affluent, fashionable holiday-makers and English families on their way to Nainital sometimes gave us a few annas or their stale sandwiches. More often we were pushed away with disdain.

"After a few days the railway police drove us out of the platform. So we took up abode in a nearby timber shed and began living like gypsies.

"The mountain air improved my aunt's health. Somebody suggested that we tour the neighbouring villages as wandering singers. The region had a flourishing timber market and people would be generous. One day we packed up and caught a motor-lorry for Haldwani. Then we began to roam the Terai. Afzalgadh. Laldang. Kalagadh. . .

"Cold winds raged about as we tramped stoney highways shivering in our rags. We were the saddest family in the world.

"Whenever, in the grey of dawn, or at nightfall, we had to traverse a forest path on foot, we could hear the distant roar of tigers. We often saw panthers leaping across the jungle roads. Since I could not walk, I had to be carried by one member of the family. Aunt Hurmuzi often snarled: 'Even a tiger doesn't like to eat this wretch.' I used to fervently pray, 'Please Allah, please tell a man-eater of Kumaon come out of the bush and gobble me up.'

"Once we sang at the bungalow of Corbett Saheb in Laldang. He was a kindly man. He gave us fifteen rupees and some old clothes.

"The bracing climate of the foothills cured my aunt of her disease. She refused to go back to the slums of Lucknow, so we spent many years in the uplands. Loaded with our baggage we trekked long miles, going from hamlet to hamlet. We suffered from frostbite and heatstroke. We braved rainfall and hailstorm. We camped by croc-infested mountain streams. You name the hardship. We have experienced it, not counting the constant penury. As I grew older, during long winter evenings spent in a barn, or starry summer nights under a pine, I sat by myself, a little away from my quarrelsome aunt and conquettish sister, and acquired the thinking habit. It was then that I began losing my faith in the figment of imagination called God.

"In one of the remote villages on the mountainside we came across a Catholic mission run by some Europeans. They hinted to us that if we adopt their religion and sing Urdu hymns during their missionary activities, they would send me and my aunt to their hospital, and Bajia to their famous convent school, in Nainital.

"When we came back to our shed downhill, I said to my aunt, 'Let us all become Christians. God is neither here nor there. So how does it matter? Our lives would be transformed.'

"Aunt Hurmuzi beat the daylight out of me. 'Fat lousy sow-wallowing-in-the-mud!,' she fumed. 'Look at her. She has lost a leg and is willing to lose the True Faith as well'!

"Anyway, the White nuns were very good to us. They taught us knitting and a little English. Jumman Khan entertained the inmates of the mission with his mimicry.

"Jumman Khan belonged to the caste of Bhands. He used to say that his ancestors were celebrated court jesters during the reign of the kings of Oudh. But times had changed and nobody appreciated their inimitable art. Therefore, he had to learn the trade of a barber. Even now he could mimic and mime well and remembered a few comic acts and jokes which he diligently presented at village fairs and weddings. Bajia and I sang and Aunt Hurmuzi, who had meanwhile married the poor clown, played the *dholak*.

"We earned very little in the poverty-stricken northern villages, but as I told you earlier, my aunt was frightened of falling ill again if she returned to Lucknow.

"When India became free, many forests of Terai were cut down to resettle Sikh refugees from Pakistan. The Punjabis could hardly understand or appreciate our songs or Uncle Jumman's jokes. So we trudged back to Oudh. "It was a frosty winter night. We were staying in a dilapidated Mughal caravan-serai somewhere in the backwaters of north-eastern Oudh. It was the month of Ramzan. Uncle Jumman had gone to the village mosque for the night-long Ramzan prayers and meditation. He used to come back at daybreak after eating the *sehri* sent to the mosque for wayfarers by pious Muslims of the village. He would gorge himself on the free meal, say his dawn prayers and return to the serai, grateful to his Lord who had not forsaken him in adversity.

"It was long past midnight. We three sat in the serai's gloomy, bat-ridden arcade, warming ourselves round a small fire. Suddenly a gang of highwaymen jumped into the quadrangle and rushed headlong towards my sister, brandishing their spears. Bajia had become well known in the countryside for her good looks, and they must have planned much earlier to carry her off.

"Fortunately, since it was a Ramzan night, all the travellers were wide awake, engaged in their devotions or cooking their pre-dawn meal on brick *choolahs.* They heard our terrified shrieks and ran to our rescue. Quickly they surrounded the bandits. There was a fight. Some people were injured. But the brigands were overpowered and chased away. One of them was recognised as the younger son of the local baron.

"Aunt Hurmuzi was terror-stricken. Immediately she decided to return to Lucknow. The very next morning we left for the city."

Jamila fell silent and began looking out of the window. Her narration seemed to have had a stunning effect on Farhad and Verma. Sadaf Ara was shedding copius tears.

After some minutes Verma said, "Jamila, perhaps you and your sister were not alone in your misery. Sadaf was fourteen when her mother sold her to the Thakur baron of her region. He was a sadist and a pervert. Fortunately, the old fogey died within a year and Moti managed to run away from his fortress. . ."

Farhad lighted a cigarette.

"Give us one," Rashke Qamar said nonchalantly. The young man was taken aback. Reluctantly he passed the tin of Goldflake to his mistress. She took out a cigarette, lighted it and began inhaling like a habitual smoker and a tramp. It saddened Verma. I had thought the world of this girl.

Rashke Qamar watched the men's reactions and gave a harsh laugh. "You are romantics, both of you. Well, grow up."

"Rashke," Farhad asked slowly, "why do some women become what they become?"

"I can ask the same question about some men, can't I?"

"No, I mean, about this class known as Khangies— veiled-courtesans—"

"Most of us belonged to lower middle-class families. My mother's father was a pious clerk. He had got my mother married to another pious, respectable, poor clerk like himself. My father died in a cholera epidemic. Mother became a widow at nineteen. Her parents also died and she had nobody to look after her. Eventually a lot of people began looking after her.

"Aunt Hurmuzi's husband had got involved in some murder case. He disappeared. Her in-laws called her jinxed and drove her out into the streets. She came over and joined my mother in Hussainabad. After my mother died in childbirth, poor Jamila's father never once came to see her. He is a dignitary of this city. Shouldn't we have reason to believe that the lowest of the lowly like our Uncle Jumman Khan are much better human beings?"

Jamila said, "All his life the poor man has been jeered at and ridiculed. The one-eyed fool. The stupid barber. The worthless mountebank. The world makes me sick."

"I have some idea," Farhad said thoughtfully. "Most of your uncle's fellow *bhands* are starving. Verma, do you remember Mustafa Hussain Bhand? He died a pauper, the last great comedian of Lucknow."

"I can recall him vaguely," Verma replied. "He had been invited to entertain at my aunt's wedding at Narahi."

"Had these people been born in the West, the whole world would have acclaimed them and they would have been millionaires," said Agha Farhad.

VII

Offices of the Songbirds Enterprises (Private) Ltd.
Managing Director : Shri N.K.Verma.
Ground Floor. Songbirds School of Light Music:
    Principal : Sadaf Ara Begum.
      Vice-Principal : Kumari Jalbala Lahiri.
      First Floor.

Gohar-i-Shab-Charagh - Urdu
    quarterly devoted to Life and
    Literature:

    Patron : Agha Farhad Qandhari.

    Editor : N.K. Verma.

    Assistant Editor : Miss Rashke Qamar
Lucknawi. First Floor.

Songbirds Dance and Drama Unit. First
Floor.

Residence of the Managing Director.
Second Floor.

Shri N.K. Verma reclines against a bolster on his divan-bed, writing the editorial of *Gohar-i-Shab-Charagh*. Like a devoted Hindu wife Sadaf Ara Begum is pressings the legs of her lord and master. God is in His Heaven, etc.

"Verma Saheb. O Verma Saheb."

"Hum . . ."

"Verma Saheb, I was wondering. What would happen to poor Qamrun now? Jamila was telling me that the poetesses who participate in the *Musairas* have started an agitation. They say they would not attend the *Musairas* in which Rashke Qamar is invited on account of her character not being good."

"*Mushaira*, not *musaira*, silly."

"All right. *Mushaira*. And Jamila was saying . . ."

"The poetesses must be draft. The History of Urdu-Literature bears witness to the fact that many famous courtesans, who were also talented poets, were highly respected by the connoisseurs."

"What?"

"Look, cuckoo, you are a bit of an ass. You can't understand these things. Now don't disturb me. I'm writing an important article."

Silence.

"Verma Saheb. O Verma Saheb. Once I dreamed a lovely dream. I saw in my sleep that you had married me. And Qamrun had come to visit us as Begum Farhad."

"You must have over-eaten that evening."

"But Qamrun did spend some good time with your friend. Went with him to so many grand *musairas— mushairas.* Calcutta. Delhi. Bombay. Once she told me that in Bombay she was feted by all the big, big Urdu writers and poets. Dinners. Parties. Picnics."

"Yeh. And when Master Farhad returned to Furqan Manzil, Dipti-Diptiayin gave him a thorough dressing down. Got him married to a cousin within the same month."

"That was the real tragedy."

"What's tragic about it? Shouldn't he have married a girl selected by his parents?"

"You men are bastards. Farhad Saheb should have defied his silly old parents and married our Qamrun. She had even borne him a son. I know you will do exactly the same. Whichever holy virgin Rajkumari Saubhagya Lakshmi Devi your Mataji selects for you, you'll go round the sacred fire with her."

"Sadaf, don't rattle me. Go to sleep. Don't forget you were a rustic tramp who danced and sang at village fairs. I made you what you are today. The celebrated songstress Sadaf Ara Begum. Even now you are not satisfied."

"Adopting a different name doesn't alter one's destiny. You changed Jamila's name. Has it made any difference? She is still hobbling about, moping. I am a Hindu and you made me Sadaf Ara Begum. You call Jamil-un-Nissa 'Jalbala Lahiri'. How does it matter? Whatever is pre-destined, shall come to pass."

"Pipe down."

"Is there any limit to God's injustices? In four years' time Rashke Qamar has produced two songs—out of wedlock. And Farhad Saheb's lawfully wedded wife, instead of presenting him a son and heir, has given him three worthless daughters. Everything God does is wonky. He has been running the world for too long, has it all mixed

up. Maybe He has grown senile. Verma Saheb . . . O Verma
Saheb. . ."

"Ya. . ." he said drowsily.

"When Nadir was born I advised Qamrun that she
ought to sue Farhad Saheb, his natural father. After all,
he is so rich. But the crazy woman was horrified. She said:
'Sadaf, never say such a thing to me again'. After the poor
brat died, Farhad Saheb started paying her two hundred
rupees a month. That's very odd. And now that she has
given birth to Aftab, shouldn't your friend give her four
hundred a month?"

"Idiot—Aftab is not Farhad's son."

"I know. It was that musician from Bombay you had
invited for the concert. Agha Farhad has stopped meeting
Qamrun, he is so scared of his wife. Gives the money as
a sort of pension, doesn't he? Can't he make it at least
three hundred? Poor Qamrun is very hard up these days.
Verma Saheb . . . You have fallen asleep. . ."

Verma was snoring. She covered him tenderly with a
blanket, and tiptoed out of the room.

The call-bell rang. She went to the drawing-room and
opened the door. A tall, good-looking, blue-eyed foreigner
in a dark, expensive suit stood smiling. He bowed and
said: "Agha Shab-awez at your service, Khanom," and
gave her his visiting card.

She went back to the bedroom and woke up her man.

"Verma Saheb. . . O Verma Saheb . . . Get up. Some
Agha Shab-deg has come."

"Who?"

"Agha Shab-deg, he said."

Verma looked at the card and uttered, "Agha Shab-
awez, stupid, woman."

VIII

"Where are you off to, Bajia dolled up like a film actress.
Going to meet Agha Shab-deg?"

"Jamila, don't you start imitating Sadaf and talk like
an illiterate peasant. I am going to see Dilip Kumar's latest
film *Aan* with Agha Shab-awez Shirazi."

"Well. Shah-deg seemed rather apt. Shab-awez is an
odd kind of name, anyway."

"A beautiful Iranian name. And his father had come to Calcutta from Shiraz."

"Watch out. He may also take you for a ride. Up the rose-garden-path of Shiraz, shall we say?"

"Black tongue. . . thoo. . . thoo. . ."

"Is he going to marry you?"

"Yes. He has said so."

"Has he proposed?" Jamila asked excitedly and dragged herself to the feet of her cot. Her face had lighted up with sudden happiness. Her sister stood near the trellised window, powdering her nose.

"He did. Last evening. Said he will write to me immediately after he goes back, and then call me there."

"Call you where?"

"He has his business all over. Calcutta. Tehran. Karachi. London."

"Does Verma Saheb know him well?"

"He had come to see Verma Saheb in connection with his business. That is how Sadaf told me at the radio station that a wealthy Agha had come from Calcutta, a broad-minded bachelor and fond of Hindustani music. He might even marry you, she said. The very next evening she arranged for a Songbirds session."

"I know all that. But Verma Saheb is quite upset because Sadaf introduces you to patrons through the Songbirds. The club is acquiring a bad name. People have started calling it Gay-birds."

"They stopped inviting me to *mushairas.* Can I run the household on the occasional radio programme? Farhad sends me two hundred out of bad conscience. Out of sheer sympathy Verma pays you fifty rupees as the so-called Vice-Principal of his mythical music school. Can all of us live on two-hundred-and-fifty a month? And I want to send Aftab to a good school."

"Bajia, is this Agha Sh'ab-awez—whatever, really going to marry you?"

"He has said so. And he is a gentleman."

"I have a feeling you have fallen in love with him. He is so handsome. A real charmer."

"Yeh. Matter of fact, I am madly in love with him. He is also very fond of me. Calls me his Rose of Shiraz."

"While in fact you are merely a watermelon of Lucknow. Never, for a moment, forget that."

Rashke Qamar glared at her.

"Black-tongued, evil-eyed witch. You are plain jealous of me. You never found any happiness in life. You can't see me happy. You lame bitch . . ." she screamed, stamping her foot.

"For goodness, sake, Bajia, don't be so common . . ." Jamila said mildly.

Bajia picked up her bag and stormed out of the room, fuming. She crossed the courtyard, lifted the jute curtain of the main door and hailed a cycle-rickshaw. As she got into the rickety vehicle she commanded the rickshawman grandly, "Carlton Hotel." Soon I'll be driving a Cadillac in the streets of London. *I will show them.*

PART TWO

IX

O gracious Lord, I beseech Thee, don't make me a woman in my next birth. . ." In the classroom of the Songbirds School of Light Music a girl-student was playing the tape of a folk song of Oudh sung by Sadaf Ara Begum and Kumari Jalbala Lahiri. *Don't let me be re-born as a girl, O God. . . Agle Janam mohe bitiya na keejo—*

The singers squatted on a reed mat in the verandah. Sadaf Ara was cutting vegetables. Jamila was looking vacantly in front of her. Her crutches lay beside her. Verma Saheb was not at home.

"It's the fifteenth day today. Qamrun must have reached Karachi," Sadaf said thoughtfully, peeling a potato.

"Can't say when and how she'll get there. She has gone illegally, without a passport. It's a perilous journey across the Rajasthan desert. And with a grown-up daughter in tow," Jamila replied wearily.

"Grown-up daughter! It seems only the other day when Mahpara was born," Sadaf remarked.

"Would he even recognise Bajia now with her grey hair and careworn face? The swine. Didn't write even once, leave alone call her over and marry her."

"In the beginning he did send a few letters, didn't he?" said Sadaf.

"Yeh. And after that, complete silence. And Bajia went on writing to him at all his addresses. Karachi. Tehran. London. Seventeen long years my poor sister spent waiting to hear from him. Morning and evening she stood in the doorway looking out for the postman. Several times a day she asked me, 'Any letter? Any telegram? It was heartbreaking. What an incredibly long wait."

"Yes. A very long wait," Sadaf repeated.

"When Mahpara was born, do you remember how Verma Saheb once again displayed his knack of choosing apt names? He had said, 'We'll call her Mahpara and Amrapali. One name Persian, one arty Indian. And when she goes to stay with her father in London, I'll suggest some nice English name for her then.'" Jamila laughed bitterly.

"He had explained to me that Mahpara meant a piece of the moon, since she was the daughter of Rashke Qamar— Envy of the Moon. Earlier, when he had blithely named the boys Nadir and Aftab he had told me that in Persian these names meant Unique and the Sun. I would have thought it all to be hilarious had it not been so sad. I have a feeling Verma Saheb likes to play God Whose creations go wonky. He would buy imported things for Mahpara and say to her, 'Tell your school friend your Persian Daddy has sent these for you from England.' " Sadaf wiped her tears.

"Sadaf Ara, you got my stupid, credulous sister involved with all those fake swamis and fakirs," Jamila said accusingly.

"She had pestered me no end to take her to some miracle-worker. She said, 'Jamila doesn't believe in God' so I can't confide in her. Take me to some good, genuine swami you know.' Mahpara was only a toddler when Qamrun first took me along to see one Shah Saheb. He was quite a rage those days. He said to her that some enemy had cast an evil spell on her. 'Give me three hundred rupees,' he said, 'and I'll buy some rare, esoteric incenses and things for the secret rites to dispel the effect of black magic. I shall spend forty days and nights in a cemetery doing special occult work.' I was scared when I heard all this but Qamrun went to see him again. He fleeced her well and proper, and vanished. Undaunted, she continued to seek out tantrik sadhus and all manner of bogus 'holy men'. She stopped telling me about them. I tried to dissuade her but she had this one obsession: Agha Shab-awez must somehow assume the responsibility of looking after his daughter. 'I shudder at the thought that the girl may have to lead a life like mine,' Qamrun used to tell me. 'Mahpara must go to her father. She must get married.'

"One thug said, 'Agha Shab-awez shall appear in your dream after twenty-one days, after which he shall write to you. Give me five hundred rupees for the very powerful occult rites I must perform to influence his mind. He lives across the seven seas. It's a difficult job as I'll have to make an astral journey and work on him.' Another swindler told Qamrun that she was under the seven-and-a-half-years malefic spell of Saturn. He also took a lot of money from her."

Jamila said slowly, "Once I noticed that whenever Bajia went out for her Songbirds or radio programmes she didn't wear any ornaments she had bought over the years. She said sheepishly that she had put her jewellery in the bank's locker for Mahpara's marriage. After she left for Pakistan I came to know that she had sold all her valuables and given the money to the some vagabond called 'Peer Falfal Shah'."

"Peer Falfal Shah advised her to go to Karachi," Sadaf replied.

"I wish I could get him arrested. Where is he?" Jamila asked fiercely.

"Vanished. One day Qamrun came here looking very happy. She said that Peer Falfal Shah had ordered her to go straight to Karachi. 'You'll meet your beloved. Your daughter shall meet her father. I have drawn her horoscope. The position of her planets is excellent. Take her to Pakistan. She will get married there to a high-born, rich man.' So, I say Jamila, maybe, for all we know, Qamrun might after all, come across her Agha Shab-deg. His heart might melt when he sees his lovely daughter. Or anyway, Mahpara might marry some nice man out there. Ever since both of them have left I have been praying for them. Some time the gods do hear."

"Do they? Have your gods heard you? You have been praying hard for yourself for the last twenty years."

Sadaf said nothing and continued slicing her radishes.

"Verma Saheb hasn't come yet. I must leave," Jamila said, picking up her crutches. The girl in the music room was now playing a ghazal sung by Rashke Qamar.

"Verma Saheb is very worried these days," Sadaf answered. "Ever since his father died, he's got too engrossed in his family business. He has no head for business and he is losing money. He was saying to me the other day that he may have to close down Songbirds and sell off this building."

"Where would you go then? His mother has still not accepted you."

"Wherever I am destined to go Jamila, I would go there," Sadaf replied simply.

"Put me in a rickshaw, Sadaf Ara, now I must go home and begin waiting for my sister's letter from Pakistan."

Dearest Bajia, Adaab.

You have been away more than a year and only a couple of postcards from you! Aunt Hurmuzi and I are extremely worried. Please, for goodness' sake, write in detail. Perhaps you have changed your residence, because you have not answered a single letter of mine.

I regret to inform you that Uncle Jumman died last week. Yesterday they recited the entire Quran for him in the local mosque where for the last two decades he had not missed a single congregational prayer. If I had believed in Heaven, I would have thought that now he must be happily telling his jokes to the angels. The world didn't appreciate him. The angels would.

I am also sorry to inform you that your beloved son Aftab has run away. He snatched from my wrists the pair of gold bangles you had given me, and decamped. Do you remember, he used to say he would stab Agha Farhad and abduct his daughter? Recently he had announced that he would go to Bombay and try his luck in the films. I am told that he has become a part of Bombay's underworld.

From his old haveli, Furqan Manzil, Agha Farhad has shifted to his palatial new bungalow in Butler Ganj. His eldest daughter (the one who is married to a Pakistani doctor in London) was here recently to attend the funeral of old Deputy Saheb, her grandfather. Diptiayin is very much alive. The second daughter is in Seetapur where her husband manages his father-in-law's farms. The youngest

one is married to some tycoon in Karachi. Farhad Saheb
had sent five hundred rupees for Uncle Jumman's funeral
expenses. His manager who brought the money told me all
this.

Bajia, can you recall that lampli autumn evening twenty
years ago? Your Persian playboy had gone away and we
were all trying to cheer you up as we sipped coffee in
Verma Saheb's colourful drawing-room? You had said: 'I
wonder why our Mother, our Aunt and we two were born
so luckless.' I had tried to philosophise again. I said: 'Look
at the real unfortunate ones of the world: the blind, the
disabled, dwarfs and hunchbacks. The hideously ugly.
Look at me, how I hop about on one leg. You are attractive.
You sing so well. And you are healthy. Think of the
diseased, the incurably ill, or those who get murdered or
those who die on the gallows.'

I remember that depressing evening so well. Verma
Saheb had said: 'Most women in our society usually get a
raw deal. And in order to make damn fools of them they
have been called Goddesses of Virtue and Devotion and
embodiments of self-sacrifice.'

We were always vastly impressed by Verma Saheb's
great compassion and sympathy for womankind. But he
never married Sadaf. For twenty-five long years she served
him hand and foot and the other day he discarded her like
an old shoe.

Shri Narendra Kumar Verma has married a fatso
Gujarati lady doctor. She had just come back from England
and was visiting some friends in Lucknow. Her father is a
mill-owner in Ahmedabad. Verma Saheb's Songbird
Enterprises had collapsed. He was running his family
business at a loss. He had to fold up "Gohar-i-Shab-
Charagh" as well. So perhaps he thought it best to marry
big money and go away to Ahmedabad. This happened six
months ago.

Sadaf Ara cried her eyes out. Verma Saheb had put
some money for her in the bank. She shifted to a two-room
flat and was planning to go back to her village when an
extraordinary thing happened.

An international conference on Indian folk music was
held recently in Lucknow. Sadaf and I were also invited. I
no longer have the stamina to sing, but for old times' sake

the organisers carried me in a chair to the conference hall. There I sat in a corner and looked wide-eyed at everybody and watched the proceedings. A number of foreigners had also come for the seminar. One of them was an American scholar of Urdu-Hindi. He had come to India to do some research on the folk songs of Uttar Pradesh.

Now, during the conference, when Sadaf sang her famous Kajries, this American gaped at her like a bewitched owl (I don't know if owls are bewitched, but you know what I mean). By the end of the conference he was head over heels—He took our friend to the court and married her. Must be quite a few years younger than Sadaf Ara and he adores her (Verma Saheb had once declared: 'If some feringhee falls in love with my Sarwan, I shall do him in).'

Sadaf brought her husband to our house. He is a nice, polite man. He was calling her 'Sadie' and Sadaf shyly explained: 'Terence Saheb says I remind him of Miss Sadie Thompson who is the heroine of a famous English novel.' I wish Verma Saheb could hear that. He was so fond of playing God.

A fortnight ago Sadaf left with her Terence Saheb for America. I have received her picture postcard from Paris. How I wish such a miracle would happen to you, too.

Verma's departure from Lucknow has made me a destitute. He had been regularly paying me for the 'Vice-Principalship' of his 'music school'. I shan't accept a pie from Agha Farhad, for the simple reason that I have not forgiven him. Can I ever forget what he had told Verma—that since he was so rich you were trying to blackmail him by saying that Nadir was his son? You said he was scared of his bad-tempered, aristocrat wife. I think he was scared of no one. He was merely a bastard. Devil roast him. After poor Nadir died you said, 'Look how he has repented and is sending you money every month as an act of atonement' I say, is 'atonement' ever possible? Hogwash. And you gratefully accepted the dole. You sneered at me and said I could not understand these things because being a cripple I had no experience of life. Maybe. But I understand about human dignity.

However, now I am completely bed-ridden. First I took in sewing. Now I am doing 'chikan' work for a middleman. I get terrible headaches after doing the intricate embroidery

*and the payment is incredibly low. My mind boggles at the
extent of the injustice. Anyway, the time of abject poverty,
has returned, which we once faced in the village of Terai.*

*Aunt Hurmuzi has grown so weak she has even
forgotten her priceless abuses. She is old and ailing, and
misses you and her husband and her grandchildren. Bajia,
if you are not successful in your mission in Karachi,
please come back, as soon as you can.*

Your loving sister
Jamil-un-Nissa.

The letter never reached the addressee. Bangladesh
War had broken out and all postal communication between
India and Pakistan was stopped forthwith.

X

My dear Jamila,

*I have sent you so many letters but have not heard
from you so far. I am extremely worried about you all back
home. Please see to it that Aftab regularly goes to school.
Even while I was there he had become quite a delinquent.
Tell Verma Saheb to get him a scholarship as a poor
student. And don't fret about me. I am fine and everything
will be all right, Insha-Allah.*

*I had written to you in detail but I have a feeling you
never got that letter. So I must tell you all over again.*

*While we were crossing over, in the convoy of illegal
immigrants, I was befriended by a poor Maulvi Saheb and
his wife, from Bareilly. They were on their way to join their
son in Karachi. They were kind-hearted and God-fearing.
I told them a cock-and-bull story that my husband had
deserted me and had run away to Pakistan and that I was
going to Karachi to look for him and sue him for
maintenance. I also told them the truth that I didn't know
a soul in Karachi. They asked me to stay with them till I
found my husband. I couldn't thank them enough.*

*We crossed the border at Khokrapar and entered the
desert of Sind. Eventually, we made our way to Karachi.
Maulvi Saheb's son Mohammed Lateef Khan had a tiny
quarter in Lalukhet which is a refugee colony on the
outskirts of the city. Lateef Khan worked as a chauffeur
for an American diplomat. He was good-hearted like his*

parents. His wife was a battle-axe. We had been there a week when I realised that the woman had become intensely jealous of Mahpara. I was horrified. I asked Lateef Bhai to find me a job in town as cook or housemaid as soon as he could.

One morning a party of Europeans arrived in Lalukhet in several cars loaded with movie cameras and things. They were making a TV film on Pakistan. Mahpara joined the crowd which had collected to watch the shooting. One of the Europeans began talking to her in English. He was a Frenchman with long ginger hair and drooping moustaches. He told Mahpara that she was one of the prettiest girls he had ever seen and that he would like to photograph her for a French magazine and pay her handsomely for it.

Mahpara came running to me excitedly and told me what that weird-looking man had said. He had asked her to come next morning to his five-star hotel. I thought it best first to ask Lateef Khan. I told her to say to the Frenchman that she would ring him up in the morning and let him know if she can model for him.

· When Lateef Bhai came home in the evening I told him. He is an old-fashioned Pathan and the son of an orthodox maulvi. So I wasn't surprised when he flared up and said: 'This would be your daughter's first step towards ruination. If you really wish to catch hold of your runaway husband and if you want him to look after his daughter, both of you must try to live like decent women. Don't you know what kind of photographs these Westerners take of young girls, for their magazines?'

I think he had vaguely guessed about my background. He also said that he had arranged for me to work as an ayah with a Japanese family. They were friends of his American boss. 'They would give you living quarters,' he said, 'and your convent-educated daughter can teach in a kindergarten school."

I accepted his advice and forbade Mahpara to contact the Frenchman. But early next morning when I got up I found my daughter had run away. She never came back to Lalukhet.

The Japanese couple live in a posh residential area. Mr. Negishi is the head of a Japanese firm. They have

*plenty of servants and I do not have much to do. They pay
me two hundred rupees with food. I have a small room to
myself. Mr. and Mrs. Negishi are a quiet, dignified couple.
Their children are schooling in Tokyo. Sunday mornings
Madam Kimura gives coffee parties and teaches flower
arrangement to her Western and Pakistani lady-friends—
This is also a kind of life! When I humbly salaam Madame
Kimura's elegant guests—wives of the diplomatic corps
and arrogant Begums—I marvel at them. Nobody can
possibly recognise me out here as 'Miss Rashke Qamar
Lucknawi', poet and radio singer of yesteryear.
Nevertheless, I have changed my name to Mona. A good
enough name for an ayah. Tell that to Verma Saheb.*

*Mrs. Kimura Negishi is a good woman. Through her
kitchen-Urdu and my pidgin English we manage to
converse. I have confided in her and she understands my
problems. The Japanese are a broad-minded people.
Madame allowed me to use the telephone and ring up
various places from where I felt I could learn of the
whereabouts of Mahpara's father.*

*I have come to know that Mahpara haunts big hotels
and is seen in the company of foreigners. She rings me up
once in a while but hasn't told me where she lives.*

*One morning she phoned excitedly and said that one
Agha Shirazi had come from abroad and was staying in
one of the five-star hotels she frequented. 'He might be my
Daddy,' she gushed. 'Why don't you go there and find
out?"*

*At once I asked Madame to give me a day's leave. After
years I made up my face, wore a nice sari and took an
autorickshaw to the hotel. At the reception counter I
asked the phone number of Agha Shirazi's room. The girls
looked at me in surprise because I had broken out in cold
sweat. Right then one of the receptionists said to someone:
'Sir, a lady wishes to see you."*

*I turned round and saw a young man who had come to
the counter to check out. He was no Shab-awez but a
Persian lad in his early twenties. He knew no Urdu but I
managed to ask him if he happened to know Agha Shab-
awez Shirazi. He asked, "The one who lives in London?" I
nodded. He said, "Baley, baley, Khanom! In fact, his son
was my classmate in Tehran. Are you asking for the same*

gentleman? His wife is a great friend of my mother. They used to live in Calcutta once upon a time. . ."

After which young Agha Shirazi picked up his overnight-bag and strode down to the Iran-air-coach.

I had, as usual, written a long letter to Shab-awez and was going to post it just before Mahpara's phone came. I took it out of my purse, tore it to bits and threw it in the dustbin. Now I am at peace. The long vigil is over.

Mahpara came to see me one evening, and said angrily that she was ashamed to tell her rich friends that her mother worked as a domestic servant. It brought her price down. 'Why don't you come and stay with me? I have a nice flat of my own and I am making a lot of money,' she said.

She keeps making air-dashes to Beirut and Hongkong and dresses up like a movie star. When I saw the glamour girl I couldn't quite recognise her.

The family in Lalukhet has heard about her. I can't face them. Lateef Khan often drives his Saheb to the Negishis' place. He has stopped recognising me. Can I ever convince him that I detest Mahpara's way of life?

Now that I have no Shab-awez to wait for, why don't I go and stay with my rich daughter? Didn't my mother, my aunt and myself do exactly what my daughter is doing now, albeit in a much better style? Madame Kimura tells me that in Tokyo there is a place called Ginza where thousands of Japanese girls are engaged in activities similar to Mahpara's. And they have replaced the old-fashioned, dignified geishas.

Likewise, the 'party girls' and 'call girls' of today have replaced our 'khangies' and 'tawaifs' of old. So why don't I live in comfort with Mahpara instead of slogging as an ayah? Perhaps, because, like the geishas of old Japan, we too had erected before us a bamboo-screen of false dignity, although the curtains behind which we lived were made of sack-cloth and the dignity was self-deceptive and illusory. Therefore, I am ashamed of accepting the earnings of a high-class call-girl called Mahpara Khanom. I am being illogical but then life itself has no logic about it, has it?

I am worried about Mahpara because the backlanes of Lucknow where we lived were safe and secluded, and men were not so ruthless. This modern, glittering world of today can be brutal and the men have become more vile.

The other day I managed to find the address of Agha Farhad's youngest daughter who is married to some business magnate of Karachi. I went there and saw a newly constructed three-storeyed ultra-modern mansion across the avenue. I gathered from the name-plate on its gate that it did belong to Agha Farhad's youngest son-in-law. I walked in and went straight to the front verandah. There was nobody about. I peeped in. In the hallway a young lady was bending over a white telephone. She was repeating 'Chippendale, Chippendale', whatever that meant. 'Yes, we have ordered Chippendale for the first floor. Yes, yes, we have imported everything from Europe. No, we've fired him. An interior decorator from Sweden is flying down tomorrow to do the room . . .'

Suddenly she looked up. Split image of her father. This half-sister of my Nadir covered the mouthpiece with her lily-white hands and shouted: 'Who are you? What do you want?"

I replied meekly: "Nothing Begum Saheba. I had come to see your ayah."

"Who let you in here? Go to the servants' entrance."

"Yes, Begum Saheb. Salaam, Begum Saheb," I said and strolled back to the gate.

The war has long been over but still there is no communication between Pakistan and India. I am giving this letter, along with your address, to my Madam. She will send it to Tokyo to her mother who will redirect it to India.

How are Aunt and Uncle? Convey to them my respectful salaams. My fondest love to Aftab. Remember me to Sadaf and Verma.

With lots of love,
Yours
Bajia

This letter, too, never reached the addressee. Mrs Kimura Negishi sent it to her old Mamma-san who misplaced it and forgot to redirect it to Lucknow, India.

XI

Banner headlines in the evening papers of Karachi:

SMUGGLER'S MOLL MURDERED IN COLD BLOOD

The badly slashed body of a beautiful young girl was found lying on the Clifton beach in the early hours of the morning. It is believed that the girl belonged to an international gang of smugglers. Her mother works as a housemaid with a foreign family residing in a fashionable locality. When the woman was called to the police morgue to identify the body she became hysterical and screamed: 'Verma Saheb, your Amrapali is dead. Verma Saheb, your Amarpali has been murdered . . .' This has led to the suspicion that mother and daughter were probably spies from India. It has also come to light that they had entered this country as illegal immigrants. Police are investigating.

Inside the police morgue:

"Name of the deceased's father?"

"Father . . . ? You could call him Qudrat-i-Khuda... marvel of God."

"That's a strange sort of name."

"All names are strange."

"His home town?"

"He was a citizen of the world, you may say."

"Don't try to be clever. Your home town?"

"It's a passing show. No place can be called one's own . . ."

"The wretch is feigning madness. All right. The deceased's passport number?"

"A corpse's passport number? Zero. . . Zero. . . Zero. . ."

"Stop drivelling. Show me her papers."

"A corpse's passport—ha. . . ha. . . ha . . . *The journey is tough, how long would ye sleep? Destination is hard to reach . . . Nasim! arise, and tie your sash . . . Get ready to leave, the night is short. . ."*

The woman had burst into a song. The police officers looked at her, aghast. She continued to sing:

Youth and charm, pomp and wealth,
Are matters all of numbered breaths . . .
Extinction awaits with folded hands,

> *Moment by moment, the warning comes*
> *To pack up and leave, saddle and go.*
> *Like the empty palms of a beggar am I,*
> > *bereft of all desire.*
> *Every care every care every care every care.*

She began droning like a cracked gramophone record. Tirelessly she repeated: *Destination is hard to reach, hard to reach hard to reach.* All of a sudden she started whirling like one possessed. Her long thick hair were flying about as she lolled her tongue out and swirled in a frenzy. She was Kali dancing in the crematorium of life.

The policemen caught hold of her with some effort and took her out to the ambulance van.

XII

The bearded young clerk of Noor-i-Islam Musafirkhana, Bombay, said mechanically: "Your passport, please. Pakistani or Indian?"

"No idea."

The clerk looked at her, amazed.

"Why did you think I was a Pakistani? Is it written on my forehead?"

"Well, Madam, you were looking around with obvious distrust, the way some people from the other country do when they first come here."

"I look at the whole world with distrust. For all I know you may decide that I am a spy and haul me off to the police lock-up. Or declare me insane and send me to a mental home. Or stab me to death in the dead of night and throw my corpse on the seashore. Or cheat me of all my life's savings and keep me in false hopes, or blacken my face and spit on it. Or I send you a thousands appeals and you don't write back once. Or . . . "

The clerk nervously rose from his chair to call the manager of the Travellers' Home. She waved her hand and said: "Don't panic, sonny boy. I am perfectly all right. You can see the brain specialist's certificate." She opened her purse, snapped it shut, and asked abruptly: "Can I make a telephone call?"

"Certainly."

She leafed through the telephone directory, found a number and dialled it.

"Hello. . . hello . . .may I speak to Sheikh Taoos?" she asked with great urgency.

"Speaking."

"Oh, hello Sheikh Saheb, Adaab Arz. This is . . .this is . . . Rashke Qamar. . ." her voice choked.

"Rashke Qamar—! You have appeared like the Moon of Eid!! Where were you all these years? I was told you had gone away to Karachi."

"I have just come back. This morning. Sheikh Saheb . . . when can I see you?"

More than a quarter century ago, when she came to Bombay with Agha Farhad, she had met Sheikh Taoos at literary dinners. He was the only person she knew well in the city. In those far-off days Sheikh Taoos used to dabble in Urdu literature and was a man of moderate means. Lately, he had made a lot of money in textiles and had given up writing poetry. Now he patronised his literary friends who flocked to his posh house to drink foreign liquor.

"Rashke Qamar Saheba . . . any time . . . any time which suits you. In fact, there is going to be a literary gathering at my place tomorrow evening. Come over tomorrow and have dinner with us. Where are you staying?"

"Noor-i-Islam Musafirkhana, Bhindi Bazaar."

"Oh. . ."

Pause.

Had she told him that she was staying at the Taj or at Oberoi-Sheraton, he would have said: "I'm coming right away," or that "I'll come to fetch you myself or send you my car." Now he said a trifle coldly: "Oh, I see. All right . . . Do come over at about seven-thirty or eight. You'll easily get a bus from Mohammed Ali Road. I live at Worli Seaface. Take down my address. . ."

The following evening the clerk of the Light of Islam Travellers' Home explained to her the bus route to Worli. She walked down to the bus-stop and got into the wrong bus. When she realised her mistake she got off somewhere on the way and waited for nearly an hour in the long queue till she found the right double-decker.

She said to a man sitting next to her, "Please tell me where to get off. I am going to Worli."

"Worli Naka or Haji Ali?" he asked helpfully.

"I don't know," she said nervously. It had grown quite dark. She got off at Haji Ali. It was a Thursday evening. Saint Haji Ali's famous offshore dargah was glittering with bright lights. Throngs of prosperous devotees were walking briskly along the long bridge which linked the mausoleum's tiny island to the main road. She sat down on the sea-wall and mumbled the Benediction. She recalled the sad old forest tomb of Peer Handey Shah. From shrine to shrine she had come a long way. She asked a woman the way to Worli Seaface and began walking again.

Eventually she found herself in the 16th-floor luxury apartment of Sheikh Taoos. The drawing room was full of literary people drinking Scotch whiskey. Sheikh Taoos introduced her to the guests. With her grey hair, crumpled, ordinary sari and faded personality she looked like an ill-paid municipal school-teacher. The hostess sized up her social status in a glance and was cool towards her. After some time the host politely asked her to recite a ghazal. She recited one, once composed for her by Agha Farhad.

There was the customary, formal Wah . . . Wah . . . *Subhan Allah* . . . After the lukewarm praise she was ignored. As she sat quietly in a corner, nobody bothered to talk to her. She was too unimportant and insignificant a being.

When the buffet dinner started, a burly, red-faced gentleman came towards her and handed her a plate. Rashke Qamar had noticed him earlier. Everyone was back-slapping him and calling him "good old Khan Saheb". He seemed the jovial, affable type.

"What would you like first . . .? *Pulao or qorma?*" he asked her. She thanked him silently for speaking to her. He sat down with her in a balcony overlooking the silvery Arabian Sea. Haji Ali's shrine glimmered in the watery distance.

"Lovely night," he commented and began eating heartily. Begum Taoos passed by and asked, "Are you being looked after, Miss Qamar?"

"Yes, thanks," she said primly.

Khan Saheb made small talk as they ate. Outside, the full moon had disappeared behind dark monsoon clouds. Khan Saheb looked at his watch and said, "It may start raining, and I have to be at some place at eleven o'clock. Can I give you a lift? Where are you staying?"

She told him.

"Jolly good. I am going to South Bombay. I'll take you to your hostel. But on the way I have to stop somewhere for a few minutes, if you don't mind."

They said goodnight to the Sheikhs and went downstairs. As he got into his car Khan Saheb said to her, "Qamar Saheba, I am an impresario. I deal in artistes. I have this strange feeling that you are not merely the usual kind of lady-poet. You are a performing artiste. Am I right? And please don't think I am being nosey but I also suspect that you are extremely unhappy. May I help you in some small way?"

"I am all right, thank you. Yes—I used to sing over All India Radio once upon a time."

"There you are!" he exclaimed, "I guessed right. Listen, if you like you can tell me the reason why you look so distracted. You see, Miss Qamar, as an impresario I have seen a lot of very unhappy artistes. In fact, I have ceased to be surprised by the extent of human misery."

"Kind of you, Khan Saheb. But I told you, I am fine. Just a wee bit tired because of the journey from Karachi."

The woman has a lot of self-pride. He remained quiet. They had come out on the main road.

"Let's have coffee somewhere," he suggested.

Mr. Khan did not cross-question her again. They went into a restaurant on Marine Drive and sipped their cold coffee in silence.

"My husband," she began bravely, "deserted me many years ago and ran away to England. I went to Karachi with my daughter. There I came to know that he had married again. I was staying with my relatives. They managed to find a nice boy for my daughter and got her married. Now that she is happily settled in her new home, I have come back."

The wordly-wise impresario knew that she was not telling him the truth. Gently he asked, "What do you intend doing now?"

"I'll think about it when I get back to Lucknow."

"Would you like to sing *qawwali?*"

"Qawwali?" Poor old Bhooray Khan came to her mind. She had been as luckless in life as that long-ago *qawwal*, who used to sing at village dargahs.

"Ladies' qawwali. Immensely popular these days." After Mr. Khan had said this, he realised that she was too old to sing the commercialised "filmi" *qawwalis* on the stage.

She smiled and answered, "I am long past the age of singing your kind of *qawwali*, Khan Saheb!"

"Why," he replied hollowly, "look at Shakila Bano Bhopali and the rest. They have even toured England with their parties." He saw his watch again and said, "Let's go. Just across the road."

They came out of the hotel and drove down to a theatre hall on Nariman Point. Inside, a "cabaret-mujra competition" was going on in full swing. A swarthy, plumpish girl was gyrating obscenely on the stage. She wore a golden wig and looked quite pathetic. The hall was full of odd-looking people, all men.

"I was told that this girl was good. But she hasn't a clue of belly-dancing. Can't do anything for her. Let's go." Khan Saheb said after a few minutes. They come out.

"And people buy such expensive tickets to see this . . ." Rashke Qamar asked, surprised.

"They have a lot of black money.'

It had started pouring. The sea roared across the parapet wall. A strong wind blew and Marine Drive was engulfed in a blurred, watery silence. A lone man stood smoking in the foyer, his face half hidden in the collar of his raincoat. As Rashke Qamar passed by he whispered something in French. She shrank up against her escort who said in an undertone, "Bombay's underworld is exceedingly dangerous. Let's get the hell out of here."

The stranger lurched forward, buttonholed Mr. Khan and said in broken English, "Monsieur, I am gentle home from Mauritius. Come Bombay thees morning. A tout brought me here. He peecked my pockette. I stranded. Please help."

Mr. Khan shook him off. He started running after the pair as they rushed out and got into the car. A black Cadillac glided into the porch. A notorious smuggler stepped out drunkenly, accompanied by a small-time actress and a swaggering, fierce-looking henchmen. It all looked eerily like a scene from an Indian movie. Mr. Khan started the engine and repeated: "Bombay's underworld . . . It's exceedingly dangerous."

"Khan Saheb," suddenly she blurted out "My daughter was murdered in Karachi's underworld."

Mr. Khan said quietly. "Tell me about it."

". . .So the policemen took me to their hospital and informed Mr. Negishi. He got me admitted into a mental home where I was given electric shocks. I was there for six months. Mr. Negishi bore all the expenses. When I came back to their house I learned that Mahpara's killers were still absconding.

"The Negishis were shortly to return to Tokyo. They said they would send me to an American family. I wanted to come back to Lucknow. It was then that I received a brief note scrawled by my sister Jamila, redirected to me from Kuwait. She had informed me that she was ill and penniless and with nobody to look after her. On the basis of that letter Mr. Negishi tried to get a special visa for me. But I had no passport. Diplomatic relations had not yet been restored between Pakistan and India. Mr. Negshi had to negotiate through some European embassy. After an entire year's effort he managed to obtain the necessary travel documents. He bought me an air ticket for Japan Airlines. They came to the airport to see me off. I shall remain eternally grateful to that angelic Japanese couple.

"Before leaving for India I went to the cemetery to say goodbye to my daughter. I sat by her grave among the nettles for a long time. Suddenly I saw a lot of well-dressed, important looking people converging around me. They were part of the funeral procession of some VIP who had died that morning. There were press photographers and TV cameramen and mourners carrying massive, black-ribboned wreaths. Fashionable ladies in white chiffon saris had covered their heads stylishly. They wore huge dark-glasses and light make-up and looked appropriately sad for the solemn occasion.

"I got up to go to the nearest bus-stop but the way was blocked by sleek, imported cars of the mourners. I sat down on a milestone, waiting for the procession to pass.

A begum in a white georgette sari threw a coin towards me, thinking me to be a beggar woman, and walked on, touching her delicate nose with a laced, tiny kerchief."

She fell silent.

"Madam," Mr Khan said after a long pause. "You told me you also have a son."

"I have. A lout. Somebody who had come to Karachi from Lucknow once informed me that Aftab was flourishing in Bombay as a ruffian. Ever since I have come here I am looking around frantically, hoping to catch a glimpse of my son. But such coincidences occur only in our films."

They had reached the Light of Islam Travellers' Home. Mr. Khan said, "You couldn't have brought any money from Pakistan."

"No. But I still have this gold bangle. I shall sell it tomorrow."

Mr Khan dipped his hand in his coat pocket, saying, "Next week I am taking a party of Ajmeri qawwals on a tour of the Gulf states, and have a lot of expenses to meet . . ."

Give us a pice give us a pice give us a pice. . . Rashke Qamar alias Qamrun of the country fairs chanted silently.

"Please accept this small sum from a sincere friend," Mr. Khan took out a hundred and fifty rupees from his wallet . . .

XIII

The muezzin was calling the faithful to the evening prayers in the neighbourhood mosque when she entered her courtyard. In the falling dusk she caught a glimpse of bicycle tyres and tubes hanging from the branches of the guava tree. It surprised her. Some urchins played in front of the tiny kitchen.

"Who's there?" a woman called out from the shadows. Rashke Qamar put down her luggage near the entrance and rushed in, shouting, "Jamila, Hurmuzi Khala, Jamila."

In her excitement she bashed her hands against the threshold as she went into the main room.

An extremely shrivelled Aunt Hurmuzi, curled up like thin smoke, rose from her untidy bed. Jamila's cot was lying empty. Her crutches stood in a corner of the dimly-lit room. Rashke Qamar's heart sank.

"Aunty, where is Jamila?" she gasped.

A woman came out of the kitchen and carried the luggage into the verandah. Then she wiped the perspiration from her forehead and posted herself inquisitively in the doorway, staring at the newcomer.

"Hurmuzi Khala, where is—?" Rashke Qamar repeated weakly.

"Gone to meet her Maker," the old woman replied in a matter-of-fact voice. "She had lost the use of both legs. God took pity on her and gathered her unto Himself."

"Jamila Bitiya could not move at all. My husband called a doctor who said it was the last stage of arthritis," the woman in the doorway spoke balefully. Rashke Qamar looked up at her.

"Till the last moment she waited for you. She had been dead over a year," said Hurmuzi Begum, tonelessly.

Rashke Qamar watched the old woman stonily. After some minutes she said in an emotionless voice, "You didn't even inform me."

"Batool's brother-in-law was going off to Kuwait. Jamila sent you a note through him. We don't have any relatives living abroad through whom we could correspond regularly, as other people have done these last few years."

Rashke Qamar stared at the empty cot. It's strange. I have not wept. Maybe Mahpara's death exhausted my stock of tears. Suddenly, she remembered her uncle and asked hoarsely, "Hasn't Uncle Jumman come back from the mosque?"

"He also died. Five years ago. Jamila, may her soul rest in peace, had written to you in detail about his death."

"I never got her letter. I never got any letter from anywhere."

Hurmuzi Begum. Jumman Khan. Rashke Qamar Lucknawi. Jamil-un-Nissa Begum *alias* Kumari Jalabala Lahiri. Mahpara Khanom . . . all . . . all were bogged down in a quagmire. One who is bogged down in a quagmire has no time to shed tears. One is too busy trying to pull oneself out. Jumman Khan, Jamil-un-Nissa Begum, Mahpara Khanom, all sank in the quagmire. She touched her dry eyes with the tip of her fingers.

"How, when did Jamila die, Hurmuzi Khala?" she asked after a while.

"How does one die, Bitiya? One just fizzles out. Jamila died in the dead of night. I don't remember the month and date. It was monsoon time. It was raining hard when she died. There was no money in the house. Bafati went out and borrowed twenty rupees from a neighbour. Then he thought of making a collection in the mosque. . ."

"Who is Bafati?"

"Hafizan's husband. He is a rickshaw-puller. Jamila had taken them in as tenants. After she became bed-ridden she couldn't go out to sing at Verma Saheb's club. But Verma Saheb and Sadaf Ara continued to help us. Verma got married and went away. Sadaf found some White saheb who took her away to Amreeka. . . So, Bafati decided to go to the mosque and get donations. I didn't want to bury Jamila in a pauper's grave, I said. After all, we do have some right on Agha Farhad. So I sent Bafati to his new bungalow. He was very ill himself. He sent some money through his manager who looked after the funeral arrangements."

"How do you manage now?"

"Jamila used to embroider chikan saris. She made twenty-five rupees or so every month. Fifteen rupees a month Bafati paid us as rent. After her death, instead of the rent paying, he feeds me twice a day. He has got TB pulling his cycle-rickshaw from morning to night. Fortunately, you had bought this house before you left, otherwise we would have been in the street."

All of a sudden the old woman remembered her great-niece. "Qamrun—where is Mahpara? With her father in London?"

"Mahpara is happily married in Karachi. I found a decent, highly educated young man with a good job for her and got her married."

"I can't thank Thee enough, O Merciful Lord," Hurmuzi Begum exclaimed. She sat up with a jerk and tried to get out of bed.

"What is it? Where are you going?"

"When Mahpara was born I had promised myself to offer special prayers of Thanksgiving if she got married." She bent down and started looking for her slippers.

"So where do you want to go now?"

"Must perform my ablutions."

"Lie down, Hurmuzi Khala. You can say your prayers tomorrow." Rashke Qamar pushed the old woman gently back on her bed. But Hurmuzi Begum was too excited and happy to keep still. She tried to get up again. In order to divert her mind her niece asked, "You said Agha Farhad was not well. What's wrong with him?"

"That scoundrel? He is suffering from some terminal disease. Gone to stay with his doctor son-in-law in England. His wife, younger daughter and her husband have also gone with him. Before he left he sent me two hundred rupees and a big fat sealed envelope for you. Wait. Give me the lantern."

"Tell me where it is, I'll look for it myself."

"Pull out the red trunk."

Qamrun pulled out the tin trunk from under Jamila's bed and opened it. It was full of old clothes. She began hunting for Agha Farhad's package. As she took out the clothes, underneath an old, yellowing newspaper she found the pair of plastic clips she had bought ages ago at Peer Handey Shah's fair. She picked them up and gazed at them vacantly.

Aunt Hurmuzi continued droning, "Aftab ran away to Bombay . . ."

"Yes. I know." Rashke Qamar resumed her search. She found the envelope hidden in the folds of a half-knitted sweater. The packet was quite heavy. Maybe he sent a wad of notes for me. Hopefully she broke open the seal and found a morocco-bound notebook and a letter . She began reading the letter in the dim light of the lantern.

Rashke Qamar,

I do not have words to express my sorrow at the death of Jamila, may her soul rest in peace. I didn't know your Karachi address or else I would have written to you. It's been more than twenty-six years when we parted. But I have not forgotten you. Whatever had to happen, happened, to you and me. You have been away almost six years and I have had no news of you from any source. After you left I tried to help Jamil-un-Nissa but she always refused to accept the money I sent her. I have never seen such fiery self-pride. She fought a losing battle with life and had to give in to death. I hope Allah gives her some comfort in the

*hereafter. Amen. She suffered enough under her sentence
of life.*

*Rashke, I remembered you intensely during the last
few years. I, too, am getting on. My wife is much too busy
in her joint-family politics. My daughters are all happily
married. God gave me everything, except personal
happiness. Over the years I wrote a lot of ghazals for you,
with the hope that if ever you come back and are invited
once again to the mushairas, these would be of some use
to you. Our society has become quite modern and liberal,
so there is no reason why you should not once again
become popular as a poetess— that is, if you ever come
back, or if, somehow, this notebook reaches you in Karachi.*

*What else shall I write? The doctors suspect lung
cancer. I am going to London for surgery. I don't think I'll
get well or come back alive to Lucknow. So, Rashke Qamar,
God be with you, and if possible, try to forgive me.*

Agha Farhad.

XIV

Ten rupees were left out of the hundred-and-fifty Mr Khan
had given her in Bombay. In the morning Rashke Qamar
went to the courtyard-door and out of sheer habit began
waiting for the postman. After a few minutes she realised
her foolishness and returned to the verandah. Bafati's
wife, Hafizan, was busy in the kitchen. Bafati had had his
breakfast of strong black tea and dry bread and gone out
to ply his cycle-rickshaw. His children were playing in the
lane. Inside, in the main room, Aunt Hurmuzi was
mumbling her prayers.

Rashke Qamar lingered in the verandah, wondering
what to do next. Suddenly she remembered the anthology
sent to her by Agha Farhad. She brought it out and
noticed that each last couplet contained her name "Qamar"
in it, in order to establish her authorship of the ghazals.
A drop of tear fell in the book. She thought for a while and
went in again. She changed her sari, made herself
presentable and began waiting for Bafati.

He came home panting at lunch-time. She said, "Bafati,
would you take me to Mansoor Nagar in the afternoon?"

"Yes, Bitiya, certainly," he replied.

After eating their routine food of coarse rice and pulses, they came out. She got into the rickshaw. Bafati coughed and heaved and pulled it on to the main road and started pedalling, with all his strength, towards the old city. They passed through the congested, once legendary areas— Victoria Street. Feringi Mahal. Chowk. Akbari Darwaza. Ghulam Hussain-ka-Pul. Eventually they reached an old mansion in Mansoor Nagar.

The gentleman she had come to see was fortunately at home, in his divankhana, having tea with his cronies. He was a well-to-do friend of Verma and Farhad. They used to call him Distant-ooq, or Farooque-pain-in-the-neck Qureshi.

As she hesitatingly entered the room he, too, exclaimed like Sheikh Taoos, "Aha . . . Rashke Qamar Saheba, you have appeared like the moon of Eid!"

She winced, and smiled wanely.

Mr. Qureshi sent for more tea and snacks and introduced her to his hangers-on.

She hadn't eaten properly since her return to Lucknow, and wanted to polish off everything, but checked herself.

After a while she asked, "Any *mushairas* to be held in the coming months?"

"Lots, " Mr Qureshi mumbled, his mouth full of tandoori chicken tikkas. "As a matter of fact, an All-India one is being held this Sunday at the Silver Pavilion, Qaiser Bagh. Would you like to take part in it?"

"I would love to, if you invite me."

"Er . . . As a matter of fact I am no longer on its committee. But my younger brother knows the new secretary. He can manage. Arre, Mian Taher . . ." he yelled.

Taher Mian came out of an adjoining room, wiping his face with a towel. He salaamed the lady in the gracious old Lucknow style. The gesture pleased her. For a moment she felt she was back in the old times.

"Taher Mian," his elder brother asked, "can you get Rashke Qamar Saheba invited to this *mushaira?* I used to know her in her heyday. You were a toddler then. But I remember how well she sang and how melodiously she recited her ghazals."

"Sure, Bhaijan, I can."

"When does it start?" Rashke Qamar asked, eagerly. "8 p.m. Don't worry. I'll send the car to fetch you, or shall come myself, " Taher Mian replied with enormous courtesy.

On Sunday morning she started getting ready for the *mushaira* She opened her trunk, took out all her saris and aired them in the courtyard. She mended and ironed her blouses and after great deliberation selected one which matched best with the sari she intended to wear. She bathed and dyed her hair. In the afternoon, she took out the book of Farhad's ghazals and selected a few to recite at the symposium. She expected quite a few encores. She had lost her singing voice but she could still recite poetry in her once-famous style.

She told Hafizan to get her dinner ready before sunset. The electricity had long been disconnected because of the non-payment of bills. She made up her face while it was still daylight. Then she put on a blue sari of American nylon she had bought in Karachi. Hastily she ate her rice and pulses, re-touched her make-up and began waiting for Taher Mian's car.

Eight o'clock. Eight-thirty. Nine. Ten. Eleven. Nobody came to take her to the *mushaira*.

She got up early next morning and called out to Bafati who was dusting his brand new cycle-rickshaw in the verandah.

She came out of the bedroom and sat down on a cane stool. "Bafati, do you happen to know the middleman who gave Jamila her *chikan* work?"

"Yes, Bitiya, I do."

Hafizan brought her a cup of hot black tea. She noticed the dark-brown, artistic piece of studio pottery and asked, "How did this come here? This belonged to the Verma household."

"Sadaf Bitiya gave us all her crockery and pots and pans before she left for Amreeka. They were all sold off during Jamila Bitiya's last illness. Only this cup is left," Hafizan replied sheepishly.

"When Agha Farhad came to know of Bitiya's illness he sent some money through his secretary, but she returned it," Bafati added.

"Does Agha Farhad have a secretary now?"

"He has a huge establishment," Bafati replied, diligently polishing the handles of his vehicle. "A carpet factory in Shahjehanpur. Farmlands in Seetapur. Apple orchards in the hills. Plus all the rent he collects from his ancestral property in the old city. Plus his new bungalow in Butler Gunj. Glory be to God. His ways are mysterious. So much wealth and no male heir to inherit it and carry on the family name."

Rashke Qamar looked away. In this very house in Pata Nala she had given birth to Farhad's natural son. Had he survived he would have been a strapping young man of twenty-four.

Hafizan picked up a bucket and ambled down to the water tap. Then she carried Jamila's cot into the courtyard and spread red chillies on it to dry in the sun. Rashke Qamar looked at the pathetic-looking stringed bed. Poor child. Your self-respect killed you.

"Then what happened, Bafati?"

"Farhad Saheb sent a large amount a second time. I took the money and didn't tell her. I thought I would get the best doctors for her and give her better food. If she asked me about the sudden prosperity I would say I have won a lottery or have taken a loan. But one of my children told her. She shouted her head off. With folded hands I said to her, 'Bitiya, I can't see you dying of starvation.'

"My rickshaw had broken down. She swore on my children's heads and asked me to get a new rickshaw with that money. She said, 'I am going to die, anyway. You have to support your family. You go and buy a new rickshaw right away.' I had to.

"She was so stubborn. Refused to be hospitalised till the very end. I know she died of hunger. After taking a few morsels she would say, 'I have no apetite.' Or 'tummy upset. Can't eat anymore.' She felt she was a burden on us. She earned a few rupees through her embroidery. She would do her *chikan* work by lantern-light till midnight. Isn't that the stuff saints are made of?" he said tearfully and added: "When I bought this rickshaw I went straight to Agha Farhad and told him the whole story."

He got up to go.

"Bafati, get me some *chikan* work from that middleman."

"Bitiya, why don't you sing on the radio? You used to, once. Now we are also going to have TV in Lucknow."

"Bafati, I have lost my voice. Old age, you know. Tell me, what are the rates?"

"One naya paisa for each motif of network, shadow-work and flower. Full sari for ten rupees. Heavier ones for twenty to thirty rupees. Our womenfolk grow half blind doing the same intricate embroidery on the same saris over and over again for which they are paid just twenty rupees but the saris are sold in the market for two hundred and are exported on even higher prices. When I was very ill, Hafizan, here, did this work, so I know all about it."

"Did Jamila embroider a full sari herself?"

"Bitiya, the system is this: An entire sari is not made in one household. One woman would make all the flowers. Another, in some other poor family, would do all the leaves, and so on. Jamila Bitiya used to make network buds . . ."

At ten o'clock the following morning, a beady-eyed man knocked on the courtyard door. For this house he had brought six yards of white muslin, some white thread and four unstitched kurtas. Qamrun went to the entrance enclosure, stretched her hand from behind the jute curtain, and took in the material. Silently, the man stalked on to the house next-door.

Qamrun came back to the verandah. She dusted the old settee and spread a clean bedsheet over it. Next she spread the sari on the sheet and carefully studied the floral design.

Then she threaded the needle, reclined against the wall, spread the *anchal* of the sari over her knees and began to embroider a leaf.

Suddenly, she broke down. She put her forehead on her knees and wept.

2
The Story of Catherine Bolton

I

F azal Masih is a poor, khaki-clad sweeper with a beatific smile. He works for an ill-tempered Englishwoman who lives on Mussoorie's Vincent Hill. Every evening, at sundown, he brings a fair, blue-eyed child to the Library Bazaar to "eat the air", as he puts it. He places the child on his shoulder and stands under a lamppost, watching the ebb and flow of holiday-makers. Standing motionless under a lamppost he can remind you of the Hindi couplet, *khara kabira der se, mange sab ki khair:* "Kabir has long been praying for everybody, for friends and foes alike in the marketplace of the world."

In Csarist Russia people like Fazal Masih were known as Holy Fools. Muslims call them *majzoob*—absorbed in God. Perhaps Fazal Masih is not a mystic, merely a sweeper with a very low I.Q. And he seems to dote on the little girl who looks like Shirley Temple. She is so pretty that the passers-by often stroll over to the lamppost to regain their breath and baby-talk to her. She is a quiet, well-behaved, well-dressed baby and looks like a high-born Missy Baba. Mussoorie is full of prosperous English and Scottish families.

But you can't know much about Goldilocks because Fazal Masih never speaks. He keeps gazing at the distant mists as though he is trying to find his answers there. Once, out of idle curiosity, a passer-by had asked him, "Which Saheb's daughter is she, Jamadar?" to which he had retorted, "She is my own niece, Babuji. You just let us be. . ."

The unexpected reply has amazed the newcomer from the plains, but some of the local cooks and bearers, ayahs

and coolies know that little Catherine Bolton is Martha
Masih's daughter and that her father was an English
Tommy. No matter. Such things sometimes happened.
Martha is Fazal Masih's attractive sister. In Urdu,
squirrels are fondly called Katto. Because of her playful
agility Martha is also known as "Katto Gilehri". Like her
brother, she works for Miss Celia Richmond. Her parents
had been baptised by Miss Richmond's missionary father.
Miss Richmond runs a second-grade "Europeans Only"
guest house called "Richmond" Inn, frequented by Poor
Whites and fair-skinned Anglo-Indians. No dark Eurasian
can aspire to be Miss Richmond's guest.

II

Now it came to pass that towards the end of the Second
World War, an English Tommy called Arthur Bolton was
billeted in Richmond's Inn. And he turned out to be a bit
odd. Instead of King and Country he liked to hold forth on
Truth and Conscience and Mr. Gandhi. He befriended the
Holy Fool, Fazal Masih, and spoke to him in the native
lingo. Like other British soldiers he had been taught Roman
Urdu but he also liked to hear North Indian folk songs
which Katto Gilehri sang rather well. Arthur Bolton was a
drummer in a regimental band. He would have liked to be
a famous musician but like many other artistes the lack
of opportunities had kept him unknown and poor. So,
instead of staying at the Savoy he had to make do with
crotchety old Miss Richmond's genteel hostel. Arthur went
hiking in the sun-hazed mountains and with Fazal Masih
he watched the dawn mists. He certainly was a very peculiar
sort of Cockney.

Before returning to Meerut Cantonment Arthur Bolton
told his friends at the Inn that they may never hear from
him. Even if I survive the war I may not write. "I hate
writing letters," he said candidly. However, he did send
thankyou notes, postmarked Meerut, to Miss Richmond
and her two servants, before leaving for the European
Front.

When Martha Masih, alias Katto, gave birth to a blonde
who resembled Arthur Bolton, Miss Celia Richmond was
not amused. She was not shocked either. She knew that
Martha was not a layabout. She had erred and may God

forgive her. Secretly Miss Richmond was happy. The
cherubic infant had suddenly lit up Miss Richmond's
lonely and dismal life. She felt that now she had someone
to live for. She was also an incorrigible romantic and a
snob. She invented a pucca background for the waif: "My
first cousin Col. Arthur Bolton," she told her Poor White
guests, "has been reported missing on the Western Front."
"Poor Arthur," she would add singing, "he was quite a
charmer, you know. And so handsome. He had married an
Irish peer's daughter just before coming out to India.
Shortly after he left for the Front poor Cathleen Bridget
died in childbirth. At the Military Hospital, you know, in
Peshawar. Fortunately, Arthur had given my name and
address to the authorities as his next-of-kin in India. The
Red Cross sent the little orphan to me—"

Even while getting her baptised Miss Richmond had
quite recklessly given the parents' names as "the late Col.
Arthur Bolton and Cathleen Bolton". "So help me God,"
she had said to herself crossing her fingers.

Catherine Bolton was a toddler when India became
free. Mussoorie's English population suddenly vanished.
Miss Richmond stayed on. She didn't want to wash dishes
in an inhospitable England. But being English and practical
she removed the "Europeans' Only" board from her gate.
The guest house began to flourish. Wealthy citizens of
independent India found a certain snob-value in staying
at the quaint old inn... "Ye olde England type, you know,
still run by a charming English lady," they wrote home on
their picture postcards.

Catherine Bolton was nicknamed "Chhoti Katto" by
the few locals who knew the secret. She was growing
lovelier by the day.

Rev. John Sigmore, the kindly English parson who
had baptised Catherine in 1946, had migrated to Australia
the following year. He had continued to correspond with
Miss Richmond. On Catherine's fifteenth birthday he wrote:
"I am worried about the dear child. What is her future in
India? Would you like her to become a cabaret dancer or
a fashion model or marry a heathen? Bring her over to
Australia before it's too late. . .."

Miss Richmond pondered over the matter. What indeed
was to become of this exquisite Eurasian girl? Was she to

join the ranks of telephone operators, office secretaries or, God forbid, cabaret dancers? Tongues had already started wagging about Catherine Bolton's exuberent vitality.

The Hindi teacher in Catherine's school happened to be a local rogue. One frosty evening he tried to kiss her and was fiercely rebuffed. He called her a tart and a "cheap mongrel". Catherine rushed home in tears and told her Aunt Celia.

That freezing December evening Miss Richmond made up her mind. She spent a restless night dreading the unknown tomorrows that were to dawn in the Australian outback. But go away she must for the sake of dear Catherine. She was very tell them. She summoned them to her room in the morning and steeled herself to make the grim announcement. Catherine sat by the fireside sorting out Elvis Persely records. The moment the servants came in Miss Richmond dropped the bombshell. "Martha . . ." (she reserved the ayah's Christian name for important occasions), "we are going away to Vilayet. Katy Baba and I. Do not worry. I'll give both of you excellent chits."

Both Katto and her brother were dumbfounded. They gaped at the bird-like Miss Saheb. Miss Richmond knitted away furiously. Katto broke down. After some moments she wiped her tears and said defiantly, "Miss Saheb. Katy is my own flesh and blood. I shan't let her go. How can you. . . how . . .?"

"Shut up!" Miss Richmond snapped in her high-pitched voice. "You are forgetting your place, Katto. Kindly remember who you are. Besides, what proof do you have that Catherine Baba is your daughter?"

Katto was horrified. The sharp-tongued Miss Saheb had never been so callous. The poor ayah began to sobheartbroken by now.

There was too much hysteria in the gloomy, Victorian bedroom. Catherine got up and went out. The very existence of her mother and uncle had begun to embarrass her since her last birthday when Miss Richmond had shrewdly told her the truth. "Col. Bolton, Cathleen Bolton and her father, the Irish lord, are entirely fictitious. But remember, some truths are not worth bandying about. You must keep your real parentage a dark secret."

Catherine instinctively knew the rules for the struggle for survival. She had followed Aunt Celia's advice.

After she left the room, Miss Richmond said more reasonably, "Think coolly, Katto. What would happen to Catherine Baba after I die? Suppose more people get to know that she is your child? Who would marry an untouchable woman's daughter—even if she looks like a European? Tell me, eh? Besides, the natives have scant respect for crossbreeds. What will she do for a living? Would you like her to take off her clothes, one by one, and dance naked in a hotel? God forbid!" she added shuddering. "Or, would you marry her off to the head jamadar of the municipality?"

Poor Katto had no answer for that.

Miss Richmond sold the guest house to a Sindhi businessman. She was still there when he took possession. He replaced Jesus and Marry with Shankar-Parvati and Guru Nanak in the lounge; "Richmond's Inn" gave way to "The New Himalaya Vegetarian Hotel" at the gate. So the day arrived when the emigrants' train pulled out of Dehra Dun railway station. Katto and her brother were left standing on an empty platform. Fazal Masih rubbed his eyes and resumed staring at the gathering mists. . .

III

Miss Celia Richmond alighted at Sydney airport and was thrilled. At last she had arrived in a White country. (She was born in Gorakhpur and had spent only six months in England.) She waited for someone to pick up her luggage. When nobody took any notice of her, Catherine brought a trolley and asked her to help. As Miss Richmond began pushing the luggage cart, suddenly she felt that the end had come.

Rev. John Sigmore was waiting in the airport verandah. He drove them home. Miss Richmond had already transferred her assets from India. The clergyman had bought her a modest flat and a grocery shop in his suburban parish. Soon Miss Richmond found herself behind a counter selling vegetables. She had become part of Sydney's working class.

Catherine joined a school and began dating. She came home late. Miss Richmond was of missionary stock and old-fashioned. "Aunt" and "niece" began to quarrel. An uprooted, middle-class English spinster and a rootless Anglo-Indian teenager made a sad and lonely pair indeed. Miss Richmond died after a couple of years. Life in exile had killed her. Catherine was not yet twenty-one when her godfather and guardian, Rev. Sigmore, died too. As a woman of means Catherine Bolton attracted crooks and hangers on. She began to live in style, in keeping with her fictitious "upperclass British" background. One of her boyfriends was a bookie. Through him she lost most of her legacy at the races. She had to sell her flat and shop to pay the debts. She desperately wanted to become an actress. There was no film industry in Australia. "The shortest cut to London's show business is through the nightclubs," a boyfriend told her. She learned cabaret dancing and got a job in a shady joint. She needed the money.

Years went by. As "Catriona the Sizzling Stripper" Catherine Bolton eventually landed up in the Hongkong-Singapore-Kuala Lumpur nightclub circuit. She could never behave like a hardened mullatto. The imaginary Col. Bolton always told her to live with a certain dignity. She remembered her doting mother and uncle and her affectionate Aunt Celia and had bouts of depression and self-pity.

Life as a taxi-dancer and nightclub hostess humbled and saddened her. At stag parties she entertained corrupt political leaders and businessmen of what was now being called the "Third World". Which was her own world? She wondered, flitting from hotel to hotel, dealing with lecherous men of all nationalities.

In every hotel room she found the same massive *Bible* on the bedside table. How much had the *Bible* helped the world, she wondered.

In Jakarta she met a Dutch sufi— thickset, blond and magnetic. He had come to Jakarta to study Indonesian Sufism, he told her. He was a "Dutch sensitive" and explained to her all about E.S.P. and Islamic mysticism. "Your father is still alive," he declared one evening. "And he is a remarkable man."

"Where is he? What does he do?" she asked eagerly.

"Can't tell you more. I can only see that he is alive; and

I can also sense that he is a great man."

"Great man?" she repeated excitedly.

So perhaps he was really a colonel and may now have become a general in the British Army. The idea that he was still around somewhere suddenly made her feel less insecure. The Dutchman's bulky presence was quite reassuring too.

Pretty soon she found herself in a mosque. An Indonesian 'sheikh' converted her to Islam and married her to Mohammad Mueen Koot of Amsterdam. She saw her new name on the nikah register and felt good: Halimawati binte Col. Arthur Bolton.

Mr. M. Koot was a strict Muslim. He forbade her to dance semi-naked in floor shows. And since his money order had not arrived from Amsterdam, she had to pay his hotel bills too. Once again she ran through most of her savings.

A month passed. One sunny morning Catherine Koot woke up to discover that the Dutch "sufi" had vanished— along with her jewellery and cash. An empty plastic cup lay on the bedside *Bible* which suddenly reminded her: Only last evening her learned husband had quoted an American author. It was something to the effect that you may roam the earth but a day comes when you realise that the world is full of Holiday Inns and plastic cups, and that you must eventually return home . . .

Catherine Koot, too, managed to return to Sydney. She was aging fast and could only become a bus conductor.

Never give up hope: is the basic rule for the struggle for survival. Catherine Koot handled the bus tickets and wondered—Maybe at the next busstop the Prince Charming. . .

IV

Raja Sir Narendranath Bajpai's ancestor was a poor Brahmin astrologer who had once pleased Emperor Jehangir with his predictions and received a jagir in the Jamuna Valley. The present Raja Saheb lived in his modern mansion in New Delhi and ran an export business. His son and heir, formerly Yuvraj Shailendranathjee (now plain Mr. S.N. Bajpai), had come out on a business tour of

Japan, South-east Asia and Australia. The Prince was not frightfully intelligent and Australia was the first White country he had ever visited. Therefore, he had gone gaw-gaw.

One Sunday morning the Rajkumar decided to see the India-Australia test match, studied the route map and boarded a Stadium-bound bus.

The coach was full of good-lookers—Lebanese, Greeks, Italians. Moon-faced Australians. But the bus conductor simply dazed him.

He blinked. She smiled politely and ambled on. The smile encouraged him. He remembered the Indian maxim about women—*Hansi to phasi.* If she smiles, it means that she is gawe. He took the same bus at the same time every day till he succeeded in introducing himself as Prince Shailendra of India.

She had met a lot of young princes in her school in Mussoorie. As a former nightclub hostess she could also distinguish between a real prince and a fake. She accepted his dinner invitation.

Our Rajas and Nawabs used to keep at least one European woman (often a Cockney barmaid) in their harems. Catherine Bolton had an impeccable background. Father British colonel. Maternal grandfather Irish peer.

As a young widower Prince Shailendra was fancy-free. He proposed to Catherine. The following week she found herself in a Hindu ashram in Sydney. In Jakarta an Indonesian sheikh had turned her into Halimawati. Down Under the South Indian swami called her Akhandsowbhagyavati Rajyalakshmi Shailaja Devijee. On the Ashram's marriage register she signed her new name: Shailaja Devi, daughter of Col & Mrs. Arthur Bolton.

V

Corporal Arthur Bolton returned home a few weeks before V-E Day— after which he was demobbed. His father— a bootblack in Piccadilly Circus—had died during the Blitz. His mother had died earlier. He had no relatives, no home. So Jesus claimed him. He found a job with a dance band in the East End, and continued to meditate in empty churches. He never married. Years passed (*A thousand*

years in Thy sight are like an evening gone). He grew old.
His left arm was paralysed. So he become a janitor. Because
of his wartime knowledge of Urdu he got along famously
with Pakistani and Sikh labourers of the neighbourhood.
One of them got him a job as a doorman at a showroom in
Knightsbridge. The shop was owned by an NRI tycoon.

Everybody in the department store liked Arthur, the
lovable, cranky old man who preached the Gospel whenever
he could.

One day during lunch-break, he sat thumbing though
the Indian glossies which lay on a counter. He glance fell
on a woman's magazine published from Bombay. The
cover girl had an English face and a titled Hindu name:
Rajkumari Shailaja Devijee.

There was an article inside. Arthur began to read:

*The Yuvrani belongs to British aristocracy. She was
born in Mussoorie. Her father, Col. Arthur Bolton, was
reported missing during the Second World War. Her mother
was an Irish noblewoman. At sixteen Catherine Bolton
accompanied her aunt, Lady Richmond, to Australia where
she learned the ballet and interior decoration.*

Arthur was dumbfounded. He retired to a corner and
read the article again and again till he got a headache.
Then he closed his eyes and began to pray.

Somehow he had a feeling that Katto was still in
Mussoorie. He wrote to her in Roman Urdu. She would get
the letter read out to her.

He received a prompt reply and applied for a month's
leave which was granted. He took out his life's savings
from the bank, got his Indian visa and air ticket and began
shopping for Katto, Catherine, and Fazal Masih. He trudged
from shop to shop carrying the heavy shopping bags
which he found hard to manage with one hand.

A few days later he was standing before the New
Himalaya Vegetarian Hotel in a warm, overcrowded and
shoddy-looking Mussoorie.

Katto tried to dissuade him. "Saheb, take my advice.
Don't go to Delhi. Katy got married and returned to India
and didn't inform me. Obviously she doesn't want to ruin
her new life. You keep out of her life too . . ." Katto was
sitting in front of the old servants quarters, placidly oiling

her hair. Fazal Masih squatted under a nearby pine, watching the mists.

"Martha, you have no anger, no bitterness?" Arthur asked, surprised.

"Anger for what, Saheb? It was all written in my fate. Just as my daughter was destined to marry a prince. It's all one's kismet, Saheb. But don't you go to see her in Delhi."

He laughed lightly and said, "Well, Martha. It seems to be written in my kismet that I go to see my daughter and you come along with me. Look at the things I've brought for her..." With childlike excitement he opened the Selfridges shopping bags.

VI

It was a cool and pleasant Sunday morning. Raja Narendranath, his younger son Gajendra, and some guests sat on the tiny front lawn listening to the discourse of a dazzling swamiji. The suave godman was a new arrival on the international guru circuit but had already become so busy that he could only come here for brunch. He had just returned from Paris with his French desciples and was staying at the Ashoka Hotel.

The swami was holding forth on Sat, Chit, and Anand when a taxi arrived at the gate. Three persons came out. One of them, a bedraggled servant in khaki, hid himself behind a magnolia tree near the gate. A seedy-looking foreigner and a shabbily dressed Indian woman crossed the lawn. The woman glanced around like a frightened squirrel.

The Raja frowned. How did the sentries let this riff-raff in? Obviously they were Jehovah's Witnesses . . . Awful bores, but harmless.

The swami paused to sip milk out of a crested glass of dull silver. "Good morning, ladies and gentlemen," the White foreigner said, grinning. The Raja beckoned them to sit down.

The old Englishman leaned forward and began listening, with rapt attention, to the discourse. When the swami paused again to let a French girl change the tape, the newcomer abruptly addressed him. "Mr. Guru," he said beaming, "I am vastly impressed by your ideas on Truth and Non-Truth. I have also come all the way from England to throw light on a certain verity. Your Highness," he turned towards the host, "your dear daughter-in-law Catherine—" he took out the magazine's cover page from his pocket, "Rajya Lakshmi Shailaja Devijee—happens to be my daughter."

"Oh, what a pleasant surprize, Colonel," the Raja cried and shook hands with him. "Why didn't you say so earlier?"

"Your Highness . . ." old Arthur replied with an angelic smile, "I am not a colonel. My father was a cobbler, my mother a charwoman. I was a drummer in the army and then in a cheap dance hall in London's East End. Now I work as a doorman."

The Raja looked aghast. The audience was frozen. Arthur glanced around and shrugged his shoulder. "This," he uttered sadly, "has always been my problem: Truth. But I was happy to find that Mr. Guru here was also talking about Truth . . ."

The audience remained frozen. Arthur changed the subject. "Sir," he said to the Raja, "Indian fathers give a lot of dowry to their daughters. I am a poor man and couldn't bring much for my child." He picked up the bags and looked around. There was no response. He put them down again on the grass. The place had become colder than the North Pole.

Undaunted, Arthur Bolton continued, "I am sure Catherine would be delighted to meet her mother. Martha was very nervous about coming here. I said, Katto, are you afraid of Light? We are all God's children. Let's go forth and meet our daughter. Can any parents and their offspring be afraid of meeting one another? That would be utterly unnatural."

The old man was absolutely crazy. The Raja stared at him incredulously. Arthur Bolton continued, "I, too, had some misgivings about Your Highness, that you may be arrogant and so on. But at the gate I overheard you saying that one should always worship Truth, and so on. I was very pleased. My Saviour had said the same thing. For the sake of Truth He got Himself crucified. It's a well-known incident. You must have heard about it."

The man was quite batty, the Raja's younger son Prince Gajendra thought and noticed with alarm that his short-tempered, august father was about to explode. "Tea or Coffee?" hastily he asked Martha Katto.

"Ah, I am also glad to see that you do not believe in untouchability. Let me introduce: This is Martha Barkat Masih, *alias* Katto, Catherine's mother. We are not legally married. One of God's great mysteries. I didn't even know about Catherine till last month when I happened to see this magazine. Martha is a brave woman. Still works as an ayah. She is a good woman. A true Christian. Her parents were pure Christians too. They were very poor. Humble sweepers, you know. Jesus said the poor shall inherit the Kingdom of God. Your Mr. Gandhi said the same thing. He lived in the Bongi Colony in Delhi. Our Martha is a Bongi too. She too will go straight to Heaven . . ."

The Raja looked horrified as he fixed his stare at the peculiar foreigner. Suddenly he held his head in both hands and screamed. He suffered from high blood pressure but nobody had ever seen him in such a state. Probably his B.P. had shot up. He felt giddy and lurched forward. Gajendra rushed in to phone the doctor.

VII

Catherine's bedroom window overlooked the tiny lawn and the front gate. She had been watching the bizzare scene from behind the curtain. The lawn looked like a stage set. The conversation sounded unreal. Such things do not happen in day-to-day life. The morning had begun as a nightmare. At the breakfast table the California-based swami and Catherine Bajpai had instantly recognised each other. It was a bizzare co-incidence. The former Hindi teacher of her Mussoorie school had obviously done very well for himself, but so had she. He had whispered to her "Listen carefully, Chhoti Katto. It's a highly competitive market for us swamis. Today I have many flourishing ashrams and thousands of disciples—all White, Wealthy and Gullible. You don't tell a soul about my past and I won't inform this Brahmin royal family that you are a sweepress's daughter."

Catherine was petrified. Discreetly she went to her bedroom while the swami strode out to the lawn to begin his lecture. And then, to her utter horror, she saw her mother arrive, followed by her dotty uncle and a tottering old Englishman.

Catherine Bajpai had overheard each and every word uttered by her improbable father, "Mad as March Hare," Miss Richmond had called him. He was worse. He was a self-righteous old fool, hellbent on ruining his daughter's life. Perhaps he also saw Visions and heard Voices. She clenched her fists in helpless rage. The people assembled on the lawn looked like characters in a farce. The bogus swami. The French disciples who were trying to escape Mahathagini Maya— the swindling World of Illusion— and had been trapped by a crooked "godman". The scowling, haughty Raja. The timid, sad-faced ayah. The incredible old Cockney from London. All her life she had wondered about her father. This was how he was destined to turn up. Now he looked extremely bewildered and worried. He looked so unhappy and so adorable—a foolish angel who had come to the wrong place and talked too damn much. The whole thing was heartbreaking. Her eyes filled with sudden tears. With a pang she felt an upsurge of filial love for the poor nut. She had an urge to go out and embrace her cranky old father, her long-suffering mother, her potty uncle. She must say goodbye to this super-fine aristocratic Brahmin family and go away with these humble, crazy, loving, poor people. She belonged with them. They were her Old Folk. The world is not only full of Holiday Inns and plastic cups. It's also brimming over with Heinz-style mansions and crested silver. And some day one must eventually return home. Am I really Akhandsobhagyawati Rajyalakshmi Shailaja Devi? I am just plain old Catherine Bolton—former taxi-dancer and bus conductor. Today at long last the tug-of-war between Col. and Corporal Bolton is also over. I must go out and announce: Dad. Mamma. Here I am. I am coming home with you.

Summoning all her courage she walked rapidly towards the door. But as she raised her right hand to open the latch, her glance fell upon her diamond bracelet. Outside, her Mercedes sparkled in the sun, suddenly reminding

her that at eleven she had to go to the Golf Club. Is all this
to vanish in an instant?

Her husband began singing in the bathroom. She
must leave herself, with dignity, before he bloody well
kicks her out. In a few minutes he too will come to know
about her mother. She must go.

The thought made her dizzy and she got hold of the
doorknob. She stood on a sinking ship. One must make
the last effort to save oneself—the second rule in the
Struggle for Survival.

Rajkumar Shailendra came out of the shower whistling.
"Why are they having this hulla-balloo outside?" he asked
in sing-song Indian-English.

She breathed deeply and said in a firm voice, "Darling,
my photograph and interview in that magazine, remember?
It was a mistake. A couple of thugs have turned up, posing
as my parents. The usual kind of blackmail, you know.
Your Pitaji is going to contest the elections. Maybe in
order to take away the Brahmin vote, his political
opponents coached a Harijan woman to come here and
declare that she is my mother. This old codger is pretending
to be my father. He may even be CIA. Call the police at
once . . ."

Prince Shailendra was not frightfully bright. But he
was not a half-wit either. He had a good look at the ashen
face of his gorgeous wife. Instead of telephoning the police
he dashed out to see his august father who was still in a
state of shock. Catherine rushed into the bathroom and
locked herself in.

At the gate her foolish uncle Fazal Masih stands
motionless, hands outstreched like Saint Kabir, praying
for friends and foes alike.

3
Confessions of St. Flora of Georgia

F irst of all, I praise Thee, O Lord, and praise Thy only Begotten Son, who raised me from the dead and is about to send me back to sleep till the Day of Judgement. Great is Thy power, O God and Thy wisdom infinite. And before Thy Throne I confess my sins committed and uncommitted and beg Thy mercy and forgiveness. O Lord my God, thou knowest well that I was re-awakened unawares. I knew not what time, day, week, month, year or century it was. I lay dead in my open coffin when a silvery wing of one of Thine angels brushed past my dusty bones and I got up. My skull was lying at my feet. I picked it up, shook off its dust and fitted it on my neck. It was pitch dark, therefore the skull was fixed in reverse. With considerable difficulty I corrected its position, and O Merciful God, I do confess that at that moment my very first desire was to find a mirror and look at myself. I glanced around and saw that a number of stone coffins lined the ancient walls of the crypt, and that the coffins were full of yellow skulls and bones. I grew very scared and trembled with Thy fear when, suddenly, the small window of the underground cell lit up with a heavenly light and the angel appeared again. Breezily he uttered, "I forgot my rosary over here. And pray, who are you?"

"Saint Flora Sabina of Georgia," I replied gravely.

"The Lord's blessings shower upon you," quoth he and began to look for his rosary. Then it came to pass that perchance my glance fell on the missing object. It was made of tiny stars and lay sparkling on the damp floor, behind a heap of bones. Promptly I said to the heavenly visitor, "You are such an angel, if I find your lost rosary for you, what would you give me in return?" He looked terribly upset. He was a very young angel. Almost a cherub.

"In the front office of St. Peter," he replied, "I have to account for each and every bead I tell. I am a forgetful angel. That's why for the last seventy thousand years, I have had to remain a trainee cherub. Now at long last I was given my halo." Proudly he pointed at his resplendent golden head. "But now I have gone and lost my rosary."

"What will you give?" I repeated.

"What do you want?"

"I died young. I was only nineteen when my father shut me up in a convent in the desert of Syria. I spent the next twenty-five years confined within the high walls of various nunneries. I do want to see a bit of the world, and crave to wear pretty clothes."

"I am not entitled to bestow on you flesh and blood. That will happen only on the Day of Reckoning. But I can ask that you be allowed to remain alive for one year."

"Angel-child, how would my poor skeleton knock about in the wide, wicked world all by itself? Could you revive some interesting corpse for me, as my companion?"

"What is an interesting corpse?" he asked.

"I mean . . ."

"All right. First give me my rosary."

"No. First revive a companion for me. Say, Arise by the Grace of Jesus."

"You are a saint. Why don't you perform a miracle or two yourself?" he replied irritably.

"Can't. There is a technical reason for it. Please say, 'Arise . . .'"

He knelt down and began to pray. Suddenly the bones started rattling in the coffin next to mine. Another skeleton got up. The angel said to me, "Remember, only for twelve months. Next year, the same month, date and time . . . eleven thirty p.m. God be with both of you . . ."

The crypt turned dark again. But now I was no longer afraid. The other skeleton stretched its claws and groped for something at the head of the coffin as though it had been his habit, on waking up, to light a candle and start reading. I addressed him and quickly explained to him the whole matter. Then a bit shyly, I asked him his name.

"Father Gregory Orbiliani of Georgia," he said, still puzzled and rubbing his sockets.

"The Lord bless you, Father," said I, and modestly added that I was St. Flora of Georgia.

"A saint . . .?" he exclaimed nervously, and jumped out of his casket. He tried to kneel before me but his knee-caps had almost crumbled to dust, so he staggered and fell down. O Gracious Lord, I prayed to Thee that if Thou hath given me this escort for a year, make his frame whole and strong. Father got up at once as a shining new skeleton. A gust of bitterly cold wind entered the window and cut through our bones. Father Gregory said respectfully, "Holy Mother, let's get out of here and try to find some warmth."

"If we could find a flint somewhere." I chattered through my teeth. Father looked out of the window where tall pine trees rustled in the wind.

"Father, come back here or you'll catch your death of cold," I said, worried.

He returned to his casket and sat down upon its ledge. I got up and leaned out of the window in order to close the shutters. Then I saw a river flowing by. Suddenly I recalled: I had lived here in a convent on this very hill, and this river came out of the Caucasian mountains and fell into the Black Sea. And while I thus stood pondering, I saw a glittering white palace appear on the silver blue waves of the river. Suddenly I heard the Last Trumpet and fell down on my face, quivering. I was exceedingly sorry that I could not get even one year to spend in Thy beautiful world.

The Last Trumpet sounded again. Father Gregory tiptoed to the window and peeped out. Then he turned to me and said, "Your Holiness, this is a steamship and sounds its horn. Please get up."

I rose from the cold floor and joined the monk at the window. Down below, in the valley, we saw a camp aglow with many bonfires. There was much laughter and sound of stringed music. I experienced a strange sensation in my bones and felt like joining the merry-makers when the Father spoke, "Let's go out and build a fire."

We groped our way out of the crypt and stumbled into a dark tunnel. The end of the tunnel was blocked by nettles and mossy stones. However, we managed to climb out and entered the monastery garden. Right in front there loomed a huge cathedral, surrounded by magnificent oaks and pines. I began to gather dry twigs and pine cones. Under a birch we came across some litter which included paper-plates and napkins. Father picked up a little paper casket full of tiny sticks. He explained that it was called a box of matches and added, "God is with us".

We lighted a bonfire and began to warm ourselves.

O Omniscient Lord! I do not tattle, but I must inform Thee, that at that moment, I saw smoke coming out of the nostrils of Father Gregory Orbiliani of Georgia. I was vastly perturbed because only Devil and his brood spit fire and smoke, and I made the sign of Thy Cross and wondered if some evil spirit had entered Father Gregory or maybe Thy forgetful trainee angel had made a mistake.

I was startled by Father's pleasant laughter. "Your Holiness," he was saying, "This thing, which I smoke, is called a cigarette. The picnickers forgot behind a whole packet."

"How," I asked, "did you know that this object was lighted and smoke emitted through one's nostrils? This indeed is a diabolic act and you must desist from it forthwith and repent."

Father Orbiliani gently explained: "Mother Flora, American scientists have invented an apparatus which you adjust on your head before going to bed and while you are asleep your brain absorbs all manner of knowledge. Now, can you doubt the infinite wisdom and power of the Almighty, who, during my thirteen-hundred-year-long sleep made me aware of a lot of extraordinary things? Even you, in the last few hours, have come to know a bit. Listen intently to the instruments being played in the valley and tell me their names . . ."

I listened carefully and understood that the merry-markers were playing Guitar, Bailalaika, Accordion and Saxophone and were singing in the Georgian and Russian languages.

Their voices were wafted to us by the wind. A young guitarist was saying to his girlfriend, "Natasha, a bonfire on the hill! Some people had been camping there before we arrived." Then the wind changed its direction and the voice receded.

The monk reverently began, "Your Holiness. . ."

"It would be better," I interrupted, "if you do not Holiness me . . . I shall soon tell you the reason."

He was taken aback. After a moment he said, "Very well. Since we have to stay together for an entire year, we may as well tell each other the truth about ourselves. I," he added with a flourish, "am the son of the Grand Duke of Tiflis, at your service, Madame."

O Merciful Lord! I did not wish to indulge in one-upmanship but had to tell him the truth about myself. "My father," I informed him simply, "is the Byzantine Ambassador to the Imperial Sassanian Court of Iran . . ."

"Was . . ." he corrected briefly, "but from Constantinople how did you land up on this far off hill of northern Georgia?"

"When we sailed from the Bosphorus . . ." I began, "the sea was calm and the wind favourable."

Gregory Orbiliani cut me short, puffing at his cigarette. "But why did you head for the Black Sea if your father was going to Iran? Was the captain of your ship a little mad?"

"Well," I said, slightly confused, "all right, Father, shall I tell you right from the beginning?"

"Do."

I relaxed a little and began. . . "Father, you know well we Byzantinians were a very grand people. Constantinople was officially called the Second Rome. After building the Church of Santa Sophia, Justinian had exclaimed 'God! I have surpassed Your King Solomon' etc., and the glorious periods of Theodosius and Arcadius. . . our Olympic games, our unique art and so on . . ."

"You have wisely omitted Empress Theodora," Father put in dryly.

"Cleopatra and Theodora, these two tried to be a little independent and you men have not forgiven them. However. So, when the Sassanians become very powerful they occupied our province of Syria and conquered Jerusalem and carried the True Cross to Ctesiphon. Our Emperor Heraclius gave them a good fight and brought the True Cross back to the Holy Land.

When the Arabs took Jerusalem from us, Heraclius brought the True Cross to Constantinople."

Father said, "In Tiblisi, I had commanded my father's army and bravely fought the Arabs. But like you

Byzantinians, we were defeated by the Muslims. They were the new World Power and Time was siding with them . . ."

"We Byzantinians loved intrigues. Our political murders and royal scandals were world-famous," I said almost proudly. "Our kings were poisoned by their queens or heirs and our Church was all powerful and our priests overfond of hairsplitting, futile religious debates. In short, we had become a thoroughly decadent people.

"My father, Stephen Honorius, was a Court Minister and my mother, the Lady Irena Maria, a lady-in-waiting to the Empress. My oldest brother, Alexander Sylvarius, commanded the Imperial Body Guard. Our entire family was deeply involved in court intrigues and a lovely time was had by all. Our neighbour, Sergius Pelagius, who lived in the palace next door was a close friend of my father. He was a merchant prince whose ships sailed the seven seas. He also owned extensive vineyards in Salonika.

"I was engaged to be married to Sergius Pelagius's only son Theodoric Gallasis. He was very handsome and extremely brainy. One day he suddenly said to me, 'I do not wish to be part of Byzantium's corrupt society. After we get married I shall take you to our estate in Salonika. There we'll lead a quiet life in our country villa. I will read the classics, you play the harp and embroider your tapestries. How I dream of such an idyll!'

"Father, I loved the gaiety of Constantinople. I attended the court balls, wore fabulous dresses and adored the gladiators. Theodoric used to say in disgust, 'We have become Christians and have still not given up the barbarism of pagan Rome.'

"Theodoric and I were to be married in the Church of St. Sophia. A few days before the date fixed for the marriage, my father came home and happily told me that as a wedding gift the Emperor (who was also my godfather) had decided to appoint Theodoric his chief A.D.C.

"That evening Theodoric, as usual, climbed the garden wall and came to my room. I was busy putting the finishing touches to the tapestry I had embroidered for my dowry. I told him the good news. Theodoric looked highly agitated. 'Can you imagine me as the Emperor's lackey?' he fumed.

'Right now I am going to arrange for a ship to take us to Gaul. We shan't even live in Byzantium.'

"Father, I was very young and foolish and did not know then that Theodoric was one of those who were called rebels and agnostics.

"I was a spoilt child and used to having my own way. I retorted, 'I shan't even think of going to the land of the barbarians. I am going to live right here and you will stay here, too, as my husband and the King's A.D.C.'

"Suddenly he grew very quiet. After a few moments he said calmly, 'Listen Flora, I detest the Emperor, the Lords and Ladies of Byzantium, and their priests and henchmen. I would rather die than join the imperial entourage.'

"We had a heated argument. He stormed out of my room, climbed the garden wall and disappeared.

"Father, little did I know at that moment that our Bulgarian maid had hidden herself behind the damask curtains of my room and eavesdropped on our conversation. Nor did I know that the girl was, in fact, a spy planted in our household by an enemy of my father. The very next afternoon my brother Sylvarius received the imperial order to invite Theodoric Gallasis to dinner and give him a poisoned drink. Furthermore, if Sylvarius didn't do so he would be murdered likewise.

"As dusk fell, I secretly made my own plans. I sent my personal maid to Theodoric, asking him to meet me at midnight at our usual rendevouz by the sea. At the appointed hour I covered myself with a cloak, hid a dagger in a sleeve, a bag of gold coins in my waistband, and slipped out of our mansion. Theodoric was waiting for me at the embankment. He was still unaware of what had happened overnight. I told him. He did not look very upset. I fell on my knees and begged his forgiveness. I said I was thoroughly ashamed of myself and would do what he said. Let's run away at once, I pleaded. Let's elope before it's too late.' He climbed the parapet of the embankment and faced the Sea of Marmora. Then he turned towards me and said in a cool, peaceful voice: 'Lady Flora Sabina of Byzantium, I will not give you the satisfaction of getting me arrested right now and handing me over to the royal executioner. Goodbye.' Instantly, he dived in the Sea of Marmora and swam furiously away.

"A strong wind blew as I stood petrified on the embankment. I was only seventeen and stupid but at that moment I suddenly grew up and realised that in a corrupt, decaying society a time comes when human beings cease to trust one another. I had no reason to blame Theodoric for suspecting me. I had come prepared to elope with him that night. We could have escaped to Bulgaria. We could hide ourselves in the Carpathians. We could run away to the land of the Goths. We could go anywhere. But he didn't trust me. He ran away alone, leaving me behind.

"Much later, I came to know that he did succeed in reaching Gaul and from there he crossed over to Britain. I do hope the Britons ate him . . ." I wiped my tears.

Father Gregory smiled and said gently, "Lady Flora, the British are semi-barbarians but not cannibals. . . What happened next?"

"As a punishment for letting Theodoric slip away, my father was more or less banished to Ctesiphon as ambassador. The Emperor knew the Sassanians were about to declare war on the Arabs and in the ensuing turmoil our family in Ctesiphon was bound to get killed. So, after a few days we boarded a ship and headed for the Mediterranean. When we sailed from the Bosphorus the sea was calm and the wind favourable.

"The ship anchored at Antioch. We climbed the marble steps of the port and went ashore. In the town museum we saw Cleopatra's marble portrait done by some Roman sculptor. I am not being catty, Father, but I assure you that Cleo was not pretty at all. I don't know who created this myth about her beauty. She had a manly face with a thick upper lip and a harsh, stern look. However, from Antioch we went to Cyrrhus, and from there via Edessa and Nisibus at last we reached the fabulous twin city of Ctesiphon. In the imperial palace by the Tigris my father presented his credentials to the Shah of Iran, King of Kings. He was heir to Cyrus and Darius but looked such a ninny. A pale, thin, nervous-looking fellow who crouched on the diamond-studded throne behind a thin curtain. As 'Shadow of God on Earth' ordinary mortals were not supposed to see him face to face, so he usually stayed behind a curtain of transparent silk.

"The Sassanians, I was glad to notice, had become as thoroughly decadent as us Byzantians. Like Constantinople, Ctesiphon was crawling with spies and rife with court intrigues and political murders within the royal family. And what revelries! The Persians' love of pomp and grandeur was absolutely incredible and they fancied themselves to be a very superior people indeed. I soon forgot about Theodoric and began to enjoy myself in the fun-loving high society of the Sassanian capital. At one of the diplomatic receptions, I met a young Roman General. We fell in love. He proposed. I accepted . . . My parents were furious. He was a Roman Catholic. We, Greek Orthodox. At home my father shouted at me: 'We did not part ways with Rome so that now I hand you over to the Pope' . . . and so on . . .

"Then I fell for a handsome Persian . . . Father, back home we had heard that the Persians were a ferocious people with long curly beards who kept their women in seclusion and were not quite civilised—at least not as civilised as we Europeans. But here I discovered that they were so refined and urbane that even sometimes our manners appeared boorish to them. In fact, their civilisation had become overripe. Anyway, so I met this good-looking Persian boy, Dastoorzadeh Minochehr Faridoon, son of the Lord High Priest of Iran."

As I remembered Minochehr, I became very sad and fell silent. The winds continued to sing in the pines. After a few minutes Father Gregory said in the grim voice of the confessional . . . "Lady Flora, please continue, I am listening . . ."

"Father. Minochehr in Persian means Lovely Face. He was really a marvel to look at. And so suave. He called me Gul Banu which in Persian means Flora, or Lady Rose. One fine evening he said to me, 'Gul Banu— Gulchehr— Ghonche, if you do not marry me I'll drown myself in the Tigris. Let's run away to Ray and get married with the Holy Fire as our witness.'

"That was a rose-tinted evening. We sat in a rose garden. Nightingales sang as we made our plans of elopement. Perhaps a Sassanian spy eavesdropped on us, hidden behind a cypress. When I returned home I was greeted by my mother in the porch. She quietly led me to my bedroom and locked me up.

"I remained imprisoned for two days and two nights and wept incessantly, remembering Theodoric, the Roman General, Lucilius Ignatius, and the Sassanian, Dastoorzadeh Minochehr Faridoon. None of them was around to help me. On the third morning my mother unlocked the door and came in. She had been crying too, because her eyes were red and swollen. She said to me briefly, 'Please get dressed for a journey.' Then she left the room. I thought perhaps they were taking me back to Byzantium. I got up, washed my face with rose water, bathed in our Persian-style *hammam*, changed and went downstairs. Nobody spoke to me. My parents, brothers, servants, all remained tight-lipped and stony-eyed. After some time my father and brothers came out in the portico. My mother embraced me and burst into tears. Still, not a word. I was convinced that father was going to tie me to a stone and drown me in the Tigris. He was known for his cruel nature. I was trembling. Mother kissed me and said, 'God be with you child'. I descended the steps and the Persian slaves helped me climb onto the *kajaveh* tied to the hump of a she-camel. My father and brothers mounted their Arab steeds. The slaves brought out heavy chests which contained the gold and jewels of my dowry. Mother had brought them along from Constantinople. They were loaded on a pair of camels. I turned round once and saw her standing in the portal weeping.

"The caravan came out of the city gate and took the road to Syria. After a few days, we reached Damascus. During the journey my father and brothers did not say a word to me. By now I knew pretty well that as punishment for trying to elope with an infidel fire-worshipper, they were going to put me to death somewhere in the midst of a god-forsaken desert and then return home.

"We left Damascus behind and continued our journey till we reached a low, rocky hill. A Greek Orthodox convent stoop atop the highest cliff. Father got off his horse, climbed the steps and pulled the bell-rope thrice. After a few minutes the massive wooden gate creaked open and a very old Greek nun peeped out. Father said something to her

and called us up. We entered a cold, bare room with a
small window, a few wooden benches and a huge Byzantine
icon on a wall. He waited awhile in grim silence till the
Abbess came in. She was also very ancient and had been
a Byzantinian princess before her renunciation. It seemed
that my father had known her in Constantinople long
years ago. The Abbess took father to another room where
they talked for some time. Then they returned. After all
these days father spoke to me for the first time. He said
sombrely, 'Listen, my child. Whatever happened, happened.
Now it is best for you that I entrust you to Jesus Christ
and His Virgin Mother.'

"'Yes Father,' I replied bowing my head. What else
could I say? Our servants brought in the chests which
father presented to the Abbess as my dowry to the convent.
After that he rose and tried to fight back his tears. My
brothers wiped their eyes and looked away. I was going to
be a bride of Christ. My father and my three brothers knelt
down before me and said, 'Pray for us'. Quickly they got
up, bade farewell to the nuns and left. I tried hard not to
break down. Then I looked out of the window. With bowed
heads my father and brothers were riding downhill, followed
by the camels. The Greek nun locked the gate and said,
'Follow me'.

"I went into a cold dark corridor at the end of which
there was an empty cell. It had a small window with thick
iron bars. A wooden plank covered with a rough blanket of
goat hair. A black habit lay neatly folded on it. A candle-
stick, rosary, wooden cup and spoon on a stool. An icon
on the wall. Silently the nun went out and waited in the
corridor. I took off my crimson silk dress embroidered with
pearls and put on the nun's habit, then I went to the door,
handed my former dress to the nun. She vanished in the
shadows. I closed the door and knelt down before the
icon."

By this time Father Gregory had finished off half the
packet of Russian cigarettes.

"What happened next . . .?" he asked, nonchalantly.

"Those were critical times, Father. The Arabs had
become a dominant power. Our Emperor Heraclius used
to go out and give them battle and lose again and again.
Some of our pious old priests used to say that God was

angry with us and had sent the Arabs to us as a
punishment. However, I hadn't been long in the convent
when some wandering monk brought the news from
Damascus that the Sassanian Emperor had sent down his
army against the Arabs, who retaliated by attacking
Ctesiphon and put an end to the Persian Empire. Iran was
now Art of the Muslim Caliphate. Fortunately, the
Byzantine Ambassador had been recalled to Constantinople
a few days before the Fall of Ctesiphon. But by this time
Byzantium, too, had lost Egypt and Syria to the Arabs. I
was extremely worried about my brothers. They could be
sent to any of the battle-fronts where we were fighting the
Caliph's armies. I prayed all the time. In fact there was
nothing else to do but pray.

"It was strange, however, that the new government of
Syria treated us with great courtesy. We heard the Arabs
say that they were following the charter of protection their
Prophet had given to the monks of the Monastery of
St. Catherine.

"At dusk one of the nuns went up to the tower to light
the lamp. We often saw Arab caravans on their way to
Lebanon, Palestine or Egypt. The camels' bells tinkled and
the leaders of the caravans sang out in their ringing
voices. At sunset they stopped, faced the direction of
Mecca and said their evening prayers. When they passed
by our convent, one of us showed them the lamp from the
tower to light their way. They called out, 'May the Lord
Bless you, O Followers of Prophet Issa, the Spirit of Allah!'
We held the lantern aloft till the caravan was lost in the
mist.

"Wealthy Christian ladies of Jerusalem and Damascus
came to our convent to lay costly embroidered sheets over
the scargophus of St. Simon who lay buried in our church.
I often envied them their beautiful dresses.

"One sunny morning I was out on the terrace feeding
the pigeons when I saw a caravan coming uphill. It was led
by a fine young lady who rode a white horse, and carried
the banner of St. George in her left hand. She was
accompanied by two handsome young Arab officers of the
Damascus Government. A large retinue followed on
horseback and camels. She was Princess Katinka Tinatin
of Georgia. . ."

The moment I uttered the name, Father Gregory was taken aback and began nervously puffing at his cigarette. I continued . . . "She had come all the way from Georgia to pray at the grave of St. Simon. The officers of the Caliph had escorted her from Damascus. She was a tall, handsome woman and rather fond of male company, for she lingered at the gate talking to the Arab officers so long that we nuns got tired waiting for her inside the gate.

"The princess stayed with us for a couple of months. She presented a chest full of gold coins to the convent and laid a diamond-studded velvet sheet on the saint's grave. Before leaving for her country she requested the Abbess to send along with her three experienced nuns to run the convent she had built on her estate in the Caucasus. The Abbess ordered myself and two other girls to accompany the princess to Georgia. One girl was Coptic and unused to cold weather. She died of pneumonia while we were crossing the snow-covered mountains of Anatolia. The third girl was Greek and she, too, had taken the veil unwillingly. When we reached Trabizon, she left our caravan and ran away with a Greek merchant. At least that's what we heard. God knows best. When we arrived here the convent was still under construction. The princess left us here and went away to Tiflis where she mostly lived. I began to organise the religious house and took charge of its gardens and vineyards. *This* was the place. I continued to miss my family and prayed for them most of the time. One day some Greek merchants arrived in the coastal village and visited our nunnery. They, of course, did not know who I was. They told me that Constantine the Second had been murdered by his son Theodosius. Then his son Constantine Ugunatus cut off the noses of his brother Heraclius and Tiberius. A lot of priests had been crucified and my father Lord Stephen Honorius and brothers were killed in the massacre that followed.

"That night I cried my eyes out in my cell. Before daybreak I washed my face with ice water and went to the chapel. I used to look after the convent gardens. From that day I lost interest in flowers and trees, birds and butterflies and all attractive things of nature, for all of them pleased the eyes and soothed the soul. I was only destined to suffer. For hours on end I lay prostrate on the ground, fasted continuously, wore sack cloth and flogged myself. The theory of katharsis evolved by us Greeks is all hogwash, Father, pardon my language. Pain is constant and eternal.

"The legends of my piety and humility and goodness spread far and wide in Caucasia. People started coming to this convent to seek my blessings. It happened that a few patients got cured. I was baffled. Now all day long the distressed, the sick and the crippled trekked uphill, all clamouring for me to pray for them. One day a beggar suffering from some highly infectious disease came to the nunnery. I nursed him diligently. He got well. I caught his disease and died. I was nearly forty-five at the time of my death. My coffin was placed in the convent's underground crypt."

"Were you good-looking?" Father asked.

"Very."

"Me too!" he said.

O Merciful God, forgive me, but at that moment . . . I wished . . . when he was alive and was still the dashing young son of the Duke of Tiblisi, and I the fun-loving daughter of the Byzantinian Ambassador to Iran . . . I wished we had met then. But Lord, Thou knowest what is best for Thy creatures. . .

I resumed my narration. . .

"After my death pilgrims started arriving on this hill.

"Some miracles were reported. Centuries passed. At last in 1873 it was decided that after the necessary investigations, if I qualified for sainthood, my name would be included in the Russian Orthodox Calendar. My case was sent up to the Patriarch of Moscow and the inquiry began. On November 25, 1921, I was to be declared St. Sabina of Georgia—but a week before that date, the Reds closed down this convent.

"Therefore, officially, I am not Saint Flora. Otherwise, perhaps I am, God knows best. Now, Father, tell me, why did *you* become a monk? The world is made for me. Why do they give it up? Was it the same old story—disappointment in love?"

Father Gregory remained silent.

O Gracious Lord, I confess that a woman's love of gossip remains unchanged even after centuries' long sleep of death. With tremendous curiosity I asked, "*Was* it princess Katinka Tinatin who broke your heart? She was a well-known flirt, poor thing."

"Lady Flora Sabina, why must you dig up old skeletons?" he said sharply.

Ha ha ha . . .! I admired his sense of humour . . . in fact black humour . . . Nervously, he lighted another cigarette. I said, "Father too much smoking would be injurious to your lungs." Then it occurred to me that this too was black humour.

"By the way," the Father said dryly, "immediately after the Muslim conquest of Georgia, your ·pious and God-fearing Princess Katinka Tinatin married an Arab General posted with his garrison in Tiblisi."

"Good God!" I exclaimed, horrified.

"This obviously happened after your noble death," Father Orbiliani continued sarcastically. "I was the son of the Grand Duke all right but after the Arab domination I was nobody. Even earlier, I never bothered about the affairs of my dukedom. I was, what is now known as intellectually-inclined. I spent my time in the scriptorium of Tiflis and was not interested in statecraft and warfare. The Princess knew which way the wind blew. The times were favouring the Arabs, and Katinka was a shrewd politician. When I heard about her marriage to an infidel, I was deeply shocked. Then I said to myself, Gregory Orbiliani, women are not worth a second thought. There is no shortage of young women and many of them are pretty and willing. So I returned to my books. But in order to be a regular research scholar at the scriptorium, one had to join the order. So I became a monk . . . Just like that. After a few months I left for Carthage and visited the school where St. Augustine had studied. Then I went to Rome, Athens, Constantinople . . . No . . . I never met your Theodoric during my travels. He must have perished somewhere in the wilderness of Britain."

"God forbid!" I said. Father Gregory began to laugh. Then he continued, "I sailed from Trabizon and returned to Georgia. No, I never visited Princess Katinka's convent. Do you see that blue mountain across the river? There used to be a monastery on its slope. Some young monks also lived in the caves. I went there, found myself a cave and joined the Brotherhood. Many of us were scholars. At night we got together in the hall and discussed academic matters or questions of dogma. If some wandering Nestorian monk turned up from far away Trans-Oxiana, we needled him about the nature of Christ. He would say, 'The Virgin Mary is the Mother of Christ, not the Mother of God.' We retorted, 'How can you prove that?' He would retort: 'How can you prove your point of view?' If a Syrian priest arrived from Damascus he would try to convert us to the Monophysite dogma and we argued with him. Some of the Brothers grew so tired of these wranglings that they went down to Tiflis and got themselves converted to Islam.

"Anyway, I was quite happy in that hermitage with my books and my intellectual pursuits. A day before Christmas I went, as usual, to the forest to cut wood. The mountains and the trees were white with snow. Cathedral bells were ringing and rabbits and squirrels frolicked around me as I hummed a Gregorian Kontakia. The axe fell on my right foot and made a deep gash. I washed the wound with snow and bandaged it with some green leaves, picked up my load of firewood and returned to the monastery. Then I got busy in the preparation for Christmas. Before going to bed in my cave at night, I lighted the candle and picked up a book. Read a little as usual and went to sleep. By the morning I had died of what is now called tetanus. I was fifty-four at the time of my death. I don't know when and why my coffin was transferred to this crypt."

A repentant Princess Katinka might have got it transferred here—I thought, but kept quiet.

The bonfire had died down. Our skeletons began rattling in the cold wind. Father Gregory said, "Let's go and find ourselves some warm clothes."

We crossed the pine grove and reached the cathedral which was fairly modern—built by Queen Goran Dukht of Georgia in the eleventh century. Obviously it was a 'functioning church' because tall candles burned before Thine icons and a shabbily dressed, bearded saxton was snoring away on a bench in front of the Lady Chapel. We tiptoed to the backroom and found an almirah full of nuns' and monks' habits, cowls and hoods. Father Gregory stole two sets of clothes which we put on immediately.

That was when we noticed somebody moving behind the wardrobe. He was a middle-aged man with bushy grey hair, bushy eyebrows and thick glasses. He too was busy stealing a monk's habit. He sensed our presence and quickly hid himself behind a door. As quickly, we came out of the church and started running downhill. As we staggered down rattling our bones we discovered that the man now dressed as a monk was following us hotfoot. We reached the youth camp and hid ourselves in a copse. The students were busy packing up and leaving for the river front. The steamer I had seen from the crypt's window gleamed beside the wooden jetty.

Father Gregory vanished for a few minutes and returned with a knapsack. He opened it and said, "I just went into an empty tent and helped myself to these. God is with us." He poured the contents on the grass. We picked up a pair each of gloves, full boots, goggles and mufflers. His expertise of petty larceny was breathtaking. We covered ourselves with goggles, mufflers, gloves and long boots, and got ready to face the 1973rd year of Our Lord. In our present disguise, we looked like a pair of live monk and nun and nobody could guess we were skeletons.

Dawn was breaking. It was a frosty morning. We followed unnoticed the huge crowd of boys and girls on to the jetty. The river was lost in the mist. The ship sounded its siren. I smiled to myself. Only last night I had thought it to be the Last Trumpet. The youngsters began ascending the gangway, singing their community songs. We mingled in the throng, boarded the ship and sat down behind a boat on the upper deck.

Suddenly we discovered that the man with bushy grey hair, also disguised as monk, had followed us and was now crouching behind us in the corner. We remained silent. So did he. The ship began to cruise along the coast, then entered the open sea.

We were going south. Father Gregory Orbiliani and I were indifferent to sleep, hunger and the need of going to the bathroom. But our mysterious companion had had to do without food and water for forty-eight hours.

One evening the ship cast anchor in the seaport of Batumi. It seemed that Batumi was a famous health resort on the Black Sea. Father Gregory, of course, knew all about it. We got mingled in the crowds, came ashore and noticed a cop eyeing us with suspicion. We began running towards the beach. Our unknown companion followed us, panting.

Eventually, we saw a lot of motor boats in the distance. It was still quite dark and not a soul stirred on the beach. We went there. Father Gregory uttered Thy Name and untied a motor boat. Then he helped me into the seat next to him. Now I saw that the third one was hovering on the shore. God, I had always heard it said that Death chased Life. Here it was the other way round! He was shouting, "Please, please, take me along, take me along." This was the first time that he had spoken to us. Father beckoned to him to jump into the boat. He did so with the speed of lightning, as it were. Father started the engine with such ease, as though in the seventh century A.D. he used a motor boat down the river Kura on his way to Tiblisi!

The unknown man sat down near us. Father Gregory asked in his professional voice: "Beloved son, what is troubling you? Why have you been following us from the Church of Queen Goran Dukht in the hills to the seaport of Batumi?" He turned to me and said, "This is a latest model jet-boat," after which he resumed in his professional tone, "Beloved son, do tell me, what is the matter with you?"

The man whispered hoarsely, "Father, I am a dissident intellectual defecting to the West. Help me."

"West?" Father repeated and steered the boat westward. Then he asked kindly, "Bulgaria or Romania, my son?" At that moment all the knowledge of contemporary world affairs had perhaps vanished from his skull. Or maybe he was thinking of Katinka Tinatin. Anyway. The unknown man nervously replied, "Father, it seems that it's the first time you have stirred out of your monastery since Forty-five."

"In the year of Our Lord six hundred and forty five, I was living in my ancestral palace at Tiflis," Father answered gravely. Fortunately the roar of engines drowned his words and the stranger continued, "Father, the West now begins from the other side of the Wall of Berlin."

Lord, I was never known to be very bright, so I exclaimed, "I have heard of the Great Wall of China and the Gates of Alexander are right there in our own Caucasia, but where on earth is the Wall of Berlin?"

Father knudges me to keep quiet. His awareness of contemporary world had returned to his skull. He turned the boat towards the coast of Turkey (formerly known as Byzantium). As we rushed on, full speed, Father shouted to the Dissident Intellectual, "Beloved son, remember Jonah and the fish and pray to Stella Maris, our guide on the high seas."

"Amen," I said and foolishly added, "Beloved son . . . remember the Lord who guides the sail ships on stormy oceans and leads the caravans across the long Silk Road, I do hope you regularly read your Lives of the Saints."

He replied, "I only read Mallarme, Kafka and Baudelaire, Madame."

Dear God, I humbly confess that I had not heard of these saints before, so I kept quiet.

O Lord of the worlds, Thou knowest well what happened afterwards. What adventures befell us on our way to Vienna. How we were welcomed and feted there, how the Dissident Intellectual addressed press conferences, gave TV interviews, signed contracts for his books and serials, attended dinners and cocktails given in his honour.

The moment we had reached Vienna, Father Gregory had said to the Dissident Intellectual, "Kindly inform the press that Father Gregory Orbiliani and Mother Flora Sabina belong to the most ancient Georgian Order, whose members take the vow of lifelong silence. For our day-to-day requirements we shall write down what we need. Moreover, we shall not get ourselves photographed because we shun such acts of vanity."

The next morning the world press splashed the following news: "Father Gregory and Mother Flora who have escaped from Soviet Georgia, vow to remain silent."

From Vienna we were taken to Paris and London. The intellectual was having the time of his life. Father browsed in the libraries and I window-shopped. The media had respected our wishes and left us alone.

After a month, O Merciful Lord, Thou knowest that we were invited to the United States of America, where we were supposed to settle down. The committee which had sponsored our visit put us up at the New York Hilton. Now, I faced the same problem which had bothered me in the hotels of Western Europe and England. God, Thou art aware of the fact that Father and I did not eat or sleep nor used the water-closet. We neither sent for breakfast in our rooms nor did we go down for lunch or dinner. We never rang up the Room Service. But for me the biggest problem was that of the bathroom. The paper ribbons around the commodes remained intact. The towels, soap, wash-basin, bathtub were unused. When the maid came in the mornings she looked a bit surprised.

I felt awkward discussing the matter with Father Gregory. But one day I had to. He answered, chuckling, "Now I am convinced that women do have inferior brains. Look, my dear, it is so easy. This is what I always do: Cut the paper ribbon, flush the commode, wet the soap and towels."

About food we had told the Dissident Intellectual as well as our hosts everywhere that we were used to keeping long fasts and only had dry bread, cheese, an onion or two and plain water. This was sent up to our rooms. Every evening we put the stuff in paper bags and took it out next morning and threw it in a dustbin down the road.

But the real crisis occurred when Father telephoned me in my room one afternoon and said, "Our hosts have arranged for us to spend the rest of our lives in a Greek Orthodox religious house in Alaska. I must discuss the matter with you at once."

I went down to his floor. He was waiting for me in an empty lounge. He said, "I have told the host that we wish to stay with some of our immigrant Georgian relatives who live in New York. After that we would like to be on our own for a while and do some research in the libraries. I'll get in touch with our Church headquarters at 15 East 97th Street as soon as our work is over. The hosts have gladly agreed. They have given me a considerable sum for our expenses for the time being. Now we must get the hell out of here. At the earliest," Father had already started speaking in American.

So the next morning we said goodbye to our friends and checked out of the Hilton Hotel.

Father rented two adjoining rooms in an inexpensive lodging house in a suburb. He spent most of the money given to us by the hosts on buying expensive books: space flights, computer technology, international politics, etc. I bought women's magazines. One day I found Father Gregory poring over the *Playboy* magazine. When he saw me he blushed (in a manner of speaking) and said, "I was reading an interview of Saul Bellow. The journal published excellent articles, you know. . ."

He also stole a few books from the libraries and smoked incessantly in his room. He could not smoke in public for obvious reasons.

Our 12-month 'parole' was about to be over. Autumn had arrived. I could feel a certain sadness in my bones when I recalled that I had not yet been able to wear a silk dress. Father was a male chauvinist you-know-who. He had ignored my pleas to let me buy a dress. He had spent my share of the dollars, too, on his books. He often went to movies and plays and left me behind in my room with the instructions to watch TV and say my prayers.

O God! I quite forgot to tell Thee that I had asked Thy forgetful angel: suppose we are not able to return to this very crypt in Georgia on the appointed hour? He had replied: "Wherever you are, you can go to the nearest cemetery, find yourselves two empty graves, and lie therein."

Time had flown so fast. One whole year had gone by in a jiffy . . . Lord, twelve months are not enough to be in Thy beautiful exciting modern world! Father had entrusted me with the job of finding a proper graveyard. While he enjoyed himself, I went around looking for empty graves in cemeteries.

Only a few days were left for the Return and Father had almost run through the money and did not want to ring up the hosts and ask for more. They would have surely asked questions. Are you still staying with your white Russian relatives? When do you wish to join the hermitage in Alaska? and so on. Now with the few dollars left (which actually belonged to me), I told Father my last wish: I wanted to buy a pretty dress. But with that sum of money Father promptly purchased a couple of books on Arab Oil and European Common Market. I burst into tears.

He said, trying to humour me, "Lady Flora, just think of the sensation the news would create, when we go underground. . ."

I didn't applaud his pun. He continued chuckling: "Think of the speculations in the world press. And both the Americans and the Russians would think that we were double agents!" He roared with laughter. I was not amused. He added, "And the Dissident Intellectual would be suspected too, poor fellow. But the situation is such that we just cannot help . . . Come, let's go out for a bit."

We came out, took a cab and went downtown. A fashion show was being held in an exclusive store. Because of our robes no one stopped us as we went in and sat down in a back row.

The models were showing the latest Dior creations. I was spellbound. Father ogled the girls.

Suddenly I was taken aback. A tall, thin model appeared wearing a crimson evening gown with a pearl studded sash. It looked exactly like the Byzantinian dress I had taken off for the last time that cold and dreary evening in the cell of the Syrian convent, fourteen hundred years ago, and exchanged it for a nun's habit. "Women's fashions haven't changed much, have they?" Father commented dryly. "Katinka used to wear such gowns too."

I said nothing and continued staring at the model as she glided away. It must have been ann extremely expensive dress. I sighed. Father whispered to me, "Lady Flora Sabina, are you thinking what I am thinking?"

"Yes, Father."

"O.K. You go home, I'll come back later."

It was past midnight when Gregory Orbiliani knocked at my door. I peeped out. He took a package from under his robe and whispered, "After the show was over I managed to reach the backroom where this gown had been put back on its hanger. God is with us."

He went to his room and began reading the book on the Palestinian problem. I rushed towards the mirror, took off my habit, and put on the gown. It needed a lot of padding. The next morning I bought several rolls of cotton wool, needle and thread, and a pair of scissors and spent the next two days in my room, diligently padding the Dior gown. After the necessary alterations when I put it on, it did not look as if it was worn by a skeleton.

It was our last day on earth. Father came home in the afternoon. We went to a nearby park and sat down on a bench. Father continued to look at me with deep sadness. Then he took out a book from his pocket and said, "Lady Flora, today I stole this from a library. This is W.B. Yeats, the Irish poet." Red leaves floated around us. It was growing dark. The sun was behind the maples. Father opened the book and said,
"Listen to this. It is called:

Sailing to Byzantium
That is no country for old men. The young,
In one another's arms, birds in the trees. . ."

As he read the poem, I remembered Byzantium and burst into tears. I was crying copiously. Father closed the book and sighed. Then he said, " On the town for the last time. . . !"

On the way to town we saw a placard announcing a masked ball in aid of Israel. It was to be held that evening in a nearby hotel. "Let's have some fun," Father said.

Before leaving the park I had put on my black robe over the silk gown. We went into a store and bought a pair of masks and wigs. Then we went in the store's cloakrooms, and got ready for the ball. Before coming out of the shop Father bought a packet of expensive cigarettes. "Save some money for the cab fare to the graveyard," I reminded him. 'It is our last evening on earth."

We walked down to the hotel, and bought the tickets for the ball. At the door Father said gravely, "The Princess Katinka Tinatin of Georgia and the Grand Duke of Tiflis   . . ."

The footmen thought us to be White Russians and looked quite impressed when he announced our names.

We entered the hall and sat down on a sofa. After a few minutes Father excused himself and went to the Men's room to smoke. I kept sitting there and thought: Only after three hours the darkness and the loneliness of the grave and the long sleep of death till. . . till. . . Kingdom come. . .

And then my glance fell on him . . . Theodoric Gallasis of Constantinople, my fiance. Doubtless it was him and none else. The same curly golden hair, the same gorgeous

Greek nose. He was disguised as a Roman senator and was dancing with a "Spanish Gypsy". I could not believe my sockets. How was it possible? Another miracle! Stunned, I gaped at him as he went dancing past.

Probably he noticed my very visible interest in him, for my glance followed him all over the ballroom. After the waltz was over he came to me and asked me for the next dance. "Sorry, Theo. . . I. . . I have fractured my toe. . . can't dance. , . do sit down for a minute, Theo. . ." I stammered, flabbergasted. He sat down. I croaked, "Are you. . . are you, by any chance Theodoric Gallasis of Constantinople?"

"No, Ma'm," he replied politely, "Richard Cohen of Brooklyn."

Right then he was joined by his 'Spanish friend'. They talked to me for a while and went away for the next dance. Father Gregory came back, reeking of strong tobacco. He flopped next to me, looked at the clock and said coolly, "Lady Flora Sabina, it's quarter to ten. Let's go."

It was then that a horrible thought came to my skull, and I blurted out aloud, and in English, "O my God, we are done for!" Ever since we had come to the USA Father had insisted that we always speak to each other in English. This will keep us in practice, he would add.

"We are in the world for a few months. Why must I bother to learn a new language?" I was rattled. And he would answer peaceably, "Lady Flora, a person usually lives in the world for about sixty or seventy years. Quite often for much less or a little more. And for such a limited span of time he spends half his life studying hard and gains the knowledge of extremely difficult subjects, struggles, acquires all manner of experiences, suffers. And despite all his knowledge and learning and self-awareness and experience and so on, one day he suddenly dies. Now, one may have to live a few months more or a few years, it boils down to the same thing. . ."

God! One could not argue with Father Gregory Orbiliani.

In public we always talked in whispers but at that moment I was so terrified that I croaked aloud! "The time given to us— was it Greenwich or Russian? There must be at least eighteen hours' difference between the Soviet Union and America. . . And also, did he tell us the date

according to the old Russian calendar or. . .?" Suddenly
there rose a murmur from the crowd of dancers. Someone
excitedly shouted, "Gee. . . Soviet spies gone berserk! . . ."

"Arab terrorists! . . ." a woman screamed.

"Good God!" Father Gregory groaned, "What next. . ."

"This, my friend. . ." a cop said, rather dramatically, as
he came forward.

We got up and were surrounded by the masked dancers.

The officer had two other policemen with him. He said,
"The gown your girl-friend is wearing, you stole it from the
Dior collection. We have been looking for you since that
night. This gown," he added, "had been made especially
for Mrs. Jacqueline Onassis." A wave of murmur swept the
hall as everybody craned his neck to have a look at my
resplendent dress. The officer continued, We have also
been informed by various public libraries that a thief
disguised as a Russian monk has been stealing rare
books . . . Kindly come with us to the police station, both
of you . . ."

At that moment Father Gregory Orbiliani looked at me
and I looked at him. Then, slowly, we took off our gloves,
our goggles and finally removed our masks. . .

4
The Guest House

Y ou can see the picturesque guest house from the bend
of the mountain road. It has a mushy name, "Arcadia".
The hill on which it sprawls is called Mount Rose. Both
names are relics of the Raj. This used to be the heart of
plantation country, dotted with gabled hunting lodges
and road houses run by seedy Burghers. The owners of
"Arcadia" now live in the capital, down in the valley. The
hunting lodges are full of bats and the road houses now
serve arrack to the busloads of pilgrims who bypass Mount
Rose on their way to the ancient Buddha temple on the
other side of the Mountains.

At the gate of "Arcadia" there sits a quaint, old
photographer. He looks like a walrus and is always dressed
carefully in a black suit and bow tie. He also belongs to a
bygone era. He keeps his hat on and his paraphernalia on
a small table and sits on a rickety tin chair, patiently
waiting for customers. The village is not on the tourist
trail. Even Americans do not often come here. Whenever
an occasional honeymooning couple or a foreigner turns
up at the guest house the photographer picks up his
camera and hopefully walks up and down the drive. The
gardener and the photographer have made a silent pact.
In the mornings the gardener prepares a bouquet for the
bride and beckons to the old man. After breakfast the
honeymooners usually come down to stroll in the garden.
They find both the gardener and the photographer ready
to greet them.

The photographer has been here for ages. You would
never know why he does not set up shop in a bigger town.
Perhaps he cannot forsake his lake and his hills. He
seems to own them. Decade after decade he has found

himself sitting on this tin chair, watching the world go by. Earlier, the Sahib loge, their Mem loge and Baba loge used to frequent this elegant guest house, mostly sahib loge and missiya loge who came here for the weekends. There were all manner of sahibs. Planters. Arrogant members of the Colonial Service—they usually wore sola hats. Army officers. And beautiful women in picture hats. All of them indulged in merry-making. The gramophone blared out *"Tropical magic, moon of sensation, strange fascination in a black velvet sky,"* and *"It was in the Isle of Capri that I found her, beneath the shade of an old walnut tree,"* and *"We were gathering stars and a million guitars played our love song."* The photographer remembers the ancient songs backwards. They waltzed and fox-trotted in the "Arcadia" ballroom till the early hours of the mornings and gathered stars in the lake and woodland.

During the Second World War "Arcadia" was haunted by the U.S. and British army personnel, Lord Louis Mountbatten slept here. The photographer had taken his pictures.

Independence changed the scene. "Arcadia" was deserted. Once in a while a brown sahib touring the province stopped overnight with his family, or a painter or two or a writer who could afford to stay in the expensive rest house, turned up to commune with Nature or rediscover the Roots of the National Tradition. The photographer never forgot to tell them that once Somerset Maugham had also stayed here. Here was certainly the kind of atmosphere which went into the making of Miss Sadie Thompson.

Some soulful people came here looking for Inner Peace. But they found no sort of peace because Extinction travels with us. Wherever we go Extinction follows us. Extinction is our constant travelling companion.

The travellers come and go. The photographer's camera eye watches and records in profound silence.

At sundown one day, a youthful couple arrived at the guest-house. They were travelling in a hired, dusty limousine. The girl had matching luggage pieces, apparently bought in New York. The pair looked affluent and widely travelled and exuded an aura of scintillating glamour. The young man carried a massive sitar. He was immaculately dressed: churidars, silk kurta, Kashmere shawl. Golden salim shahi shoes. He had curly hair and romantic eyes. The girl was pretty and oozed self-confidence which comes with recognition and success. They seemed to belong to the show business but both the gardener and the photographer could not recognise them. However, they waited expectantly for the morning.

The pair had booked separate rooms. The bearer informed the photographer later that night. The photographer nodded with much understanding. Not Mr. and Mrs. Smith. Separate rooms. Eh? We shall see. We shall see . . .

The pair came upstairs. The upper floor was empty. The bearer took them to a large bedroom overlooking the lake. The girl threw her parasol and overnight bag on a bed.

"Hey, listen. Pick up those things and scram. This is my room," the young man said.

"O.K. chief," the girl said with mock obedience.

They crossed into a lounge beyond which there was a smaller bedroom. The bearer led her in, carrying her luggage.

Back in his room the young man uncovered the sitar and started tuning it.

"Don't show off," the girl shouted from her door and went back to opening her suitcase.

There was a roofless corridor behind the room. It seemed to be under repair. She heard a couple of labourers shouting to each other in their language. They had finished the day's work and were removing their step-ladders and tools. The girl went to the window and watched the sarong-clad men with little buns at the nape of their heads. Suddenly they left and there was intense silence. The girl had her bath, changed and came out in the lounge. Her companion had stopped tuning the instrument and stood in the bay window. She joined him and looked out. The sun had gone down. The lake looked very dark.

Then they sat down on the window seat and began to talk.

Down below, the photographer packed up for the day and caught a glimpse of two shadows looming in the upper floor window. In the blue light of the evening the lighted window looked like a large painting with a gilt frame hung on a country house wall. The two were talking excitedly and laughing. What were they discussing so eagerly? What plans were they making? The photographer got up to go down to the outhouses where he lived. The pair's voices carried to the garden in the still night. The photographer's camera eye could see, but it could not hear.

After a while the pair went into the dining room, and sat down at a window-side table. Outside, the lights of the township began to sparkle in the deep dark waters of the lake.

A European tourist arrived. Probably he was a documentary film-maker or an anthropologist or a journalist looking for Communist guerillas in the bush. One can never know what drives people to come to strange, faraway places. What do they find? What happens to them when they get back or return? Whatever becomes of them all over the world? What the hell is happening to people all over the world?

The European sat at another table under the main window. He had piled a stack of picture postcards in front of him and was briskly writing on them, one by one.

"You know what this fellow is writing home?" the young musician whispered cheerfully to the girl.

"'Wish you were here'. . . What else?"

"Yes. 'Wish you were here. I am sitting in a mysterious rest house in the depth of the mysterious East. An exotic, dark-eyed Indian beauty, . . .'"

"Eeek . . ." the girl giggled. The European looked up and smiled affectionately at the couple. Doubtless, all the world loves lovers.

After dinner they returned to the lounge. It had grown very cold. The girl sneezed. "Must go to bed," she said.

"Yes. And don't forget your cough mixture."

"Shan't. Good night."

She got up and went to her room. The corridor at the back was plunged in darkness. The room was pleasantly cool and comfortable, and full of peace.

The girl opened the top drawer of the dressing table and took out her cough mixture. There was a knock at the door. The girl put on her rustling pink and black kimono ("Brought it for a song in a back street in 'Frisco . . . last time I was there for my coast-to-coast. . . you know. . ." she airily told her envious women friends) and opened the door. The young man stood there in his Kashmere dressing gown, sneezing loudly. "Gimme that wonder medicine of yours," he said, blowing his nose.

The girl gave him the bottle along with a pink plastic spoon. The spoon fell down on the floor. The young man picked it up and sauntered back to his room.

"Lady," said the photographer darkly, "a terrible battle is raging outside. . ."

In the morning the dining hall sparkled and shone like that of a luxury-liner. The girl felt as if the next moment it may start moving. The hall was fragrant with flowers. Silent, sarong-clad servants had polished large metal vases with a lot of Brasso and placed them in a row on the polished wooden floor. Freshly cut flowers were lying in a heap near the glittering vases. Outside, the sun turned the lake into gold. Enormous butterflies, white, yellow and purple, flitted around in the garden. The girl sat down at the table and picked up the newspaper.

The young man's curly head appeared on the staircase. He carried a bunch of huge roses.

"The gardener has sent these to you, with his salaam!"

"Oh, how nice! Remind me to tip him before we leave," she said absently. Then she tucked a rose in her hair and resumed reading the newspaper.

"A funny-looking photographer was also hovering around, downstairs. He asked me, with great courtesy, if you were Filmstar Nargis!"

The girl looked up and winced.

"I'm sorry," the man laughed, "but the old fellow seems a bit dotty. Didn't recognise you. No offence meant, I'm sure." He poured coffee. "In fact, dear one, you ought to be grateful that at least here you are left alone." Then he added in a put-on theatrical manner. "No autograph hunters. No flash bulbs. No reporters."

The girl grinned and said with a flourish, "Darling, how I adore such moments of peace when I travel incognito." Both laughed.

From his table the lone European saw them and smiled. He seemed to share their moments.

After finishing breakfast the pair went downstairs. They crossed the lawn and headed for the limousine parked on the slope. Suddenly the old man materialised before them under a flaming gulmohur tree. He doffed his porkpie, bowed low and said, "Good morning, lady, sir. Photograph lady?"

The girl looked at her watch and said, "Er. . . we are off to the mountains to see the Standing Buddha or the Lying Buddha or whatever. We'll get late."

"Sleeping Buddha, lady," the photographer corrected her gently. Then he barred her way, placed one foot on a railing and waved his arm towards the world in general. "Lady," he said darkly, "A terrible battle is raging outside . . ."

"Battle. . .?" the girl repeated, alarmed.

"A battle, lady. In the Battlefield of Life."

The pair smiled indulgently. The photographer continued, "I know you have come here from the Front for a little respite. Home leave, as it were. Do you see that lake? The rainbow spans it and vanishes. Just like that. Follow me, lady," he jumped down on the lawn.

"Whew!" the girl whispered to her companion.

The gardener had been waiting for his cue. He appeared from the sundial and presented a bouquet. The girl giggled again and took the bouquet from his hand as though she were receiving it on stage.

The pair were led towards the granite statue of a plump, saucer-eyed apsara (goddess.)

"Antique?" the young man asked with interest.

"Hundred per cent. Five thousand years old. The name is Amar Sundari Parvati." The photographer made the man and woman pose beside the statue. The girl blinked in the sun and shaded her eyes with her palm. Click. Click. The picture was taken.

"Thank you, lady. Thank you, sir," the old man bobbed like a puppet. "You'll get the prints in the evening."

The young man paid him and made for the car.

They came back late in the evening, and sat for some time on the lawn. When it became frosty they moved inside. They were leaving the next day.

In the morning the bearer knocked on the girl's door. "Come in," she said. The bearer handed her a large envelope with her name scrawled on it. "The photographer had left this for you last night, mem saab."

"Thank you. Put it in that drawer please," she said absently and continued to comb her hair.

In the evening as she packed her things she forgot to open the drawer. Before leaving she looked around to see if she had left anything behind. Then she rushed downstairs.

The limousine came out of the gate. The photographer got up from his tin chair and took off his battered hat. The pair smiled and waved at him. The car disappeared behind the bend.

The thin man with the walrus moustache has grown very old and feeble. He continues to sit on his tin chair outside "Arcadia". His suit is threadbare, his hands palsied. He must earn his meagre livelihood photographing the tourists. They come in droves because of the new air service. But they come laden with their own Japanese cameras and ignore the old man who has become quite a nuisance. The lakeside village is now a flourishing hill resort.

The coach from the airport arrives at six in the evening. Being off-season, today it was almost empty except for an elderly lady who stepped out frowning. She looked intently at the old man who eagerly got up from his chair. Instead of some young and pretty girl he saw a flabby old woman and went back disappointed.

The lady went into the office and signed the register. Then she went upstairs. The guest house was empty. A party of Japanese pilgrims had just left for the temple in the mountains. The servants were tidying up the rooms. Tall vases reflected on the polished floor of the dining hall. Silver sparkled and shone under the chandelier. The newcomer crossed the empty bedroom and didn't wait for the bearer to lead her to the room across the lounge. She flung her attache to the glazed verandah where she had her tea. After a while she went into the dining room and ordered dinner.

Hurriedly she finished eating, went back to her room and flopped on the bed. She started dozing.

Soon she was disturbed by a noise and got up to investigate. She went to the window and peeped out. A new room was being added to the roofless corridor at the back. A workman who had perhaps forgotten something behind had lighted a match and was rattling and banging the cans of paint.

"Stop this racket, you fool," the lady shouted crossly. The labourer ignored her and continued his noisy search. After a few moments he disappeared in the dark. She returned to her bed.

There was a loud knock at the door. She got up grumbling and opened it. There was nobody. She peeped out into the lounge. It was empty. She shivered a little and came back to bed. The room had grown very cold. There was only one blanket.

In the morning she began packing and opened the dressing table drawer to look for her throat lozenges. She was sure she had put the packet somewhere last evening. She rummaged the empty drawer and yanked out an old newspaper. Beneath the paper she noticed a large, yellowing envelop with her name scrawled across. Surprised, she pulled it out. A cockroach jumped out of the envelope and crawled on to her finger. She screamed and shook it off. A yellow photograph slipped out of the envelope and fell on the floor. She picked it up and gazed at it as a young man and woman smiled mindlessly standing beside the statue of Amar Sundari Parvati. Then she looked around like a thief and quickly slipped the photograph in her bag.

The bearer knocked on the door. "Coach ready, mem saab," he announced.

The lady got up. The bearer came in and picked up her rather shabby luggage.

Downstairs, the photographer was hovering near the coach, angling for new arrivals. The lady went up to him and spoke with sudden familiarity. "It's extraordinary. Very. Strange. In the last 22 years," she said grimly, "the dressing table must have been dusted thousands of times. Thousands of times," she repeated. "But this picture this picture . . ." she waved the old snapshot under the scarecrow's nose, "it has been lying there for 22 years."

Her voice became harsh and peevish. "The place has vastly deteriorated. The rooms are full of cockroaches."

The old man was taken aback. He tried to recognise the middle aged, bad-tempered woman. With great sadness he looked away. Even her voice had changed. She continued irritably in a harsh monotone:

"I am . . . used to be a world-famous dancer. World-famous. Who the hell will photograph me now? Just stopped here on the way home." (Now she sounded apologetic.) "Had gone abroad for treatment. I have sciatica, you know. Here." She placed her hand at her back. "They said this Chinese pins and needles thing is good. All bogus. The new air service is awful. But it costs less if you take this shorter route. . . Everything has become so expensive. . ."

"And your...er...your friend," the old man asked in an undertone as one conspirator to another. He was embarrassed by his question but he must find out. He was also cursed with a photographic memory.

The driver honked the horn of the airlines coach.

"Who. . . he. . .? Reported Missing," she said briefly and pursed her lips.

"Eh. . . ?" The old man had grown a bit deaf but he understood.

"Lost in the Battlefield of Life, as you would put it. Reported Missing. Fell off somewhere by the roadside."

"Hurry up, Mem Sahib," the driver shouted.

"Lost long ago. Long time no see. Eh—? ha, ha. Never found again," the lady finished almost triumphantly, as though she were saying 'So, there you are!'

She nodded politely at the photographer who took off his hat and bowed low like a courtier in a pantomime. She walked briskly towards the coach. The photographer ambled down to the gate, head bent down, hands in coat pocket. He returned to his chair, crossed his legs and resumed twiddling his toes.

Life, it had devoured the humans.

Only cockroaches shall survive.

5
Beyond the Speed of Light

I

Dr. (Miss) Padma Mary Abraham Kurian. Age: 29. M.Sc. (Madras); Ph.D. (Columbia); Height: 5'2", Complexion: Olive. Eyes and hair: black. Brown mole on left temple. State: Kerala. Mother tongue: Malayalam. Religion: Syrian Church of Malabar. Personal faith: Agnostic. Profession: Government Service.

On her return from the U.S.A. Padma Mary had been working in the Space Research Centre somewhere in South India. She had been allotted a cottage on the campus, where she stayed with her college-going brothers. Both her parents were retired school teachers who lived in their hometown, Cochin. Padma was a quiet, diligent and dedicated scientist. She saw one or two films every month and once in a while invited her colleagues to have Chinese food which she loved to cook. She was saving a few hundred rupees every month in order to buy a second-hand Fiat car and went around on her old bicycle. Being a workaholic she came home late from her office. In short, she was a normal, uncomplicated, modern Indian career woman who hoped to get married before it was too late.

On a pleasant afternoon of April 1966, Padma looked at her wristwatch and realised that she was feeling hungry because she had skipped breakfast in the morning. She decided to go home for lunch.

On the way to her cottage she had to go through a coconut grove and cross a tiny bridge spanning a rivulet. This was a secluded area of the campus. Today, while she reached the bridge she caught sight of a small, unusual kind of rocket which stood glowing dimly on the turf. It gave off a strange, bluish light. Padma was intrigued. She had been reading a lot about flying saucers in the newspapers, those days. For a moment she thought no U.F.O., but an optical illusion or auto-suggestion. Being a scientist she did not believe in this nonsense of little men from outer space. She got off her bike and went closer. Then she touched the rocket's cold metal and glanced around. There was no Martians waiting to kidnap her. But the rocket-like thing was for real. Maybe some of her colleagues had constructed an experimental dummy spaceship and left it here for the time being. Must find out. She placed her hand on the door. It opened by itself. Inside, there were two seats but no pilot. Being engaged in space research herself, Dr. Kurian hopped in excitedly. The door closed. She sat down in the cockpit and examined the dashboard. Could not understand its mechanism. there were countless very tiny push buttons marked with the numerals BC-AD. The needle of the lighted dial stood still on A.D 1966

Feeling a bit scared she decided to get out. As she rose from the pilot's seat her elbow struck the push-button marked 1315 B.C. There was a flash of fierce, white light and the rocket zoomed off.

Poor Dr. Kurian was petrified. Cold sweat appeared on her brow and she experienced a momentary blackout.

When she opened her eyes, and looked out of the porthole, she saw the familiar blue sky above and a desert and the marshes of a delta down below. She heaved a sigh of relief. This was no science fiction. She was still in her own world. Thank the Good Lord . . .

The rocket landed. The red needle stopped at 1315 B.C. The automatic door opened. Padma Mary jumped out. A little goatherd sat on a stone beside the lotus-filled pond, playing his reed-pipe. His goats grazed under the date-palms. The pyramids loomed in the distance. Gosh! It was merely good old Egypt. She had visited this country on her way from New York to Bombay. She had photographed the pyramids and met the same kind of goatherd and fallaheen—this was no 1315 B.C. This was very much A.D. 1966. And this contraption was certainly no Time Machine. This must be some latest kind of space rocket which a visiting American or Soviet scientist might have brought to our Space Research Centre.

She felt at ease but the next moment she was seized by another fear. She was in Egypt without a passport and she could be arrested "loitering near a space rocket in suspicious circumstances". Egypt may be a friend of India and all that, but she must rush to her Embassy in Cairo at once.

The local people who roam around the pyramids have picked up English from the Western tourists. So she said to the little goatherd—"Bus—taxi—Cairo—" The boy shook his head. A peasant riding a donkey came along. The urchin said something to him.

Suddenly Padma had a terrible revelation. *She could understand the language in which to two Egyptians were speaking.* This was not Arabic, because she had heard the Moplah maulvis of her neighboured in Cochin loudly reciting the *Quran*. She not only understood it but she found herself speaking in this improbable North African tongue. Fluently she asked them, "Cairo—how far?"

They looked at her, askance. She still could not understand how it occurred to her that she should say "Memphis" instead of Cairo.

The peasant told her that he would take her there, on his donkey. She was feeling very hungry. It was long past lunch time. She must buy some snacks in the city. But she had no foreign exchange. In the meanwhile if these ancient, ignorant people broke up her rocket, how would she get back to her own time? She looked back and saw that a little crowd had already gathered and the villagers were lying prostrate before the time-machine. When they saw her one of them shouted, "O goddess Hathor—" The rest chorused "Hail Hathor—Mother of God, who hath come down to earth on her celestial chariot, have mercy on us—Intercede with your Son on our behalf—"

Padma remained quiet for a few minutes, thinking hard what to do. Then she said with enormous dignity:

"I am not Hathor, but an emissary of the Goddess. She had sent me down on a secret mission. Do not tell anybody about my visit or else the Goddess's wrath shall destroy you. And till I come back from town, guard well my heavenly chariot, and don't you touch it or you will drop dead."

II

Memphis was a bustling metropolis as it ought to have been. The donkey-man was trembling with fear. He had brought a celestial being, riding piggy-back on his humble animal. He quickly dropped her in the marketplace and rode off.

Padma Mary found herself standing in front of a large shop. Inside there were rolls of papyrus lined up along the walls. A very tall, attractive, young man was talking to the shopowner. He was dressed in a black- and gold-striped sarong, sported a fringe-cut and looked like a character out of a Hollywood movie about Cleopatra or the Ten Commandments. She pinched herself. This was no film set, but a noisy, dusty bazaar, with flies and moving throngs of people, all clad in "period costumes".

There must be a restaurant out here. Don't these people eat? She looked around frantically, feeling utterly famished.

The stately young man came to the door of the shop and saw her.

In any respectable science fiction, romance should start from this point. But it didn't, because Padma was much too hungry to appreciate the golden Egyptian. She moved on, looking for a foodstall and spotted two bearded men sitting on the steps of a fount. Somehow, they seemed very familiar in the weird surroundings. They wore long robes of the kind she had seen the priests of her own church of Kerala and the rabbis of the Cochin Synagogue and the Moplah maulvis wore, back home. The two old men also wore skull caps. Right then a fierce-looking man appeared from the crowd. He carried a hunter and a long piece of papyrus. He gave the paper to the old men and strode on haughtily.

One of the bearded men saw the paper and cried out plaintively:

"Mikhael ben Hannan—the chief slave-driver has come."

A young man with a long nose and sensitive features emerged from a by-lane.

"May the One True God curse these evil times. Throw dust on thy head and weep, O Mikhael, that thy name has also appeared in the list of Pyramid-builders."

Mikhael turned pale and said, "Our Lord may soften the heart of Prince Thoth. I happen to know him. That Lord God is my refuge and my succour who helped the people of the faith in the reigns of the king of Arioch, and the king of Elazar—

"Prince Thoth?" one old man whispered.

"Rabbi, I just saw him at the stationery mart. He would surely rescue me."

Michael was speaking in the most ancient language which was spoken even before the time when the earliest chapters of the Old Testament were written. This writer does not know either the ancient Coptic, or Aramaic or Syriac, or Hebrew, but it came to pass that Mary Kurian understood what Michael said. She watched the Hebrew young man enter the papyrus shop. He saluted the handsome Egyptian who said, "Hello, Mikhael! Nice to see you. What are you doing these days?"

"I work at the River Customs, Your Highness..."

"Jolly good," Prince Thoth said patronisingly. He belonged to the ruling race. The Hebrews called Apru by the Egyptians, were a persecuted minority. Now Mikhael spoke to him in an undertone. The prince raised one eyebrow and listened with dignity. "Don't worry. I'll speak to the Hon'ble Minister in charge of Housing for the Dead. Keep in touch."

Then the two young men noticed the lady standing on the footpath, gaping at them. Thoth pushed Mikhael aside with his elbow and proceeded majestically towards the strange-looking female.

Padma thought quickly: If I tell him I am an Indian dancer touring Egypt, he may take me to the slave-market and sell me off to some Middle Eastern potentate. That Hathor's hand-maiden story is better. But then he may take me to a temple and suffocate me to death with the smoke of incense. If I tell him the truth he wouldn't understand. Even I can't understand how I have turned up here.

Prince Thoth stood in front of her like a stone colossus of Abu Simbal. He asked gravely, "And why were you eavesdropping on us? Which country has sent you as a spy?— Elam—? Assyria—? Arartu?"

Padma was terrified. Thoth gazed at her sari of American nylon and her Italian bag. She said with great humility:

"O Prince— this slave-girl is dying of hunger. Please feed me first. I'll tell you the whole truth."

"Come along," he ordered. Timidly she followed him to the chariot-stand. He made her sit beside her and whipped the caparisoned horse.

They came out of the bazaar and reached the fashionable locality of Heliopolis. Tall mansions stood on either side of the street. There was a lot of garbage lying around. Children played on the footpath. The chariot stopped in front of a three-storeyed house.

A squint-eyed Nubian slave opened the crimson portal. They entered the hall. There was a tank in the midst of its gleaming floor of black tiles. Rolls of papyrus tied with golden cords lined the shelves. There were frescoes on the walls, gold powdered couches and chairs were placed around the tank. It seemed that all these things had been brought back from the British Museum's Egyptian Rooms and put here. Thoth ordered food to be served. Then he planked on a settee, took off his sandals, and twiddled his toes, looking at Padma questioningly. She sat down on the edge of a chair and said nervously, "Your Highness, I am coming from India."

". . . ?"

"I am a dancer." She rose to her feet and presented a bit of Mohiniattam she had learned in school. Then she sat down again. Thoth was not impressed.

"Sir, my sail-ship was wrecked in the Suez Canal . . ."

"Suez Canal . . ?" Thoth repeated. "What's that?"

Padma grew more jittery.

"Do you know this Apru lad?" Thoth asked irritably.

"Sir, I swear upon the Goddess Hathor and her divine son, that I do not know anybody in this country."

Thoth believed her because she had sworn upon his Mother Goddess. And she looked sincere, and scared.

"All right. Do not go on sirring me. Come along and have a bite."

He led her to the dining room. The slaves brought food in silver dishes. At ten o'clock in the morning she had just had a cup of coffee with her colleagues Dr. Rafique Fatehally and Dr. Ram Nath. This was 4.30 in the evening. Quickly she took off her wristwatch and hid it in her handbag. Then she began eating the utterly unpalatable ancient Egyptian delicacies.

The sun was setting in the river Nile and the desert wind had become cool. She was strolling with her charming host in the long verandah. By now she had come to know the following facts: Thoth's real name was Astalis. Thoth was his official designation. His father was also called Thoth, named after Thoth Hermez, the God of Libraries. The fearful statue of this god stood in the main hall, next to the mummy of a holy cat.

Mr. Thoth Senior was Chief Secretary to the Pharoah and also closely related to the Royal Family. Thoth Junior wrote and painted.

He belonged to the circle of young artists and writers of Memphis and was very much against some of the antiquated beliefs and customs of his land. He was a modern young Egyptian, but the old guard did not listen to the radical views of the New Generation.

So this is the reality of the romance of Ancient Egypt—! Padma thought with much disappointment. One of the calligraphists who was busy copying the *Book of the Dead* sneezed loudly and was constantly scratching his head. Two young scribes were quarrelling with each other. The slave-girl Anoti was no beauty. She was fat and pock-marked. Even Thoth was a normal, average kind of a young fellow, except that instead of coat and trousers he was clad in the Hollywood-style "period costume".

The Pharoah was away on the Assyrian border in order to inspect his troops. The war with Assyria had been going on for years.

"We are the world's oldest and the finest civilisation. The Chaldeans and the Assyrians say the same thing about themselves and give us battle. But it is quite obvious that they are no match to us. We are far superior to them. We are the greatest," Thoth said with great emotion. She smiled.

"But I must admit—" he added magnanimously, returning to the scriptorium, "The Chaldeans and the Assyrians are a highly educated lot— Look at these clay tablets— But they are also very cruel. Before the camel-loads of their clay books were brought here—"

He picked up a tablet in cuneiform script. "I have seen it in the British Museum—" she bit her tongue and checked herself. "Do you live here alone, Thoth?" she asked quickly. "Father has gone to the war-front with the King. My mother and sisters have accompanied the Queen to Thebes. I, too, have to go there to paint frescoes in a new wing of the palace over there. But I can't leave till I get the new edition of *The Book of the Dead* prepared. It is always in great demand because one copy of this book is entombed with each mummy. And people, as you know, have this habit of dying all the time."

"Tell me, Thoth, why are you all so fascinated by death?" she asked.

"What else should fascinate us? Mortal life?" he retorted.

They were passing along the shelves marked Religion, Ethics, Law, Medicine, Astronomy, Rhetorics, Mathematics, Geometry, Travelogue, Novel. *The Romance by Aniteph.*

"He was born thirteen hundred years ago," Thoth informed her. Padma quickly calculated and uttered "Oh! 2600 B.C.!"

"What does B.C. mean?" asked Thoth. Hastily she moved on to the next bookshelf. "We have other interests, too, besides Death! These books are copied here and sent out to the College Library at Thebes."

"I didn't know you people were so learned— I mean are so learned— *The Sayings of Tahhotep*— what does he say?" (Now, of course, she could read the hieroglyphs too.)

"He says—" Thoth pulled out a silken scroll and began reading— "Don't spread fear and terror among men. God shall punish you for this. The person who says all power and all might belongs to him, often he stumbles and falls. Always live in the House of Compassion. God is the Provider. The mortal must not feel that he can achieve anything on his own. And beware! Never spread mischief through words!"

She moved on towards the row of copyists sitting on the floor. She knelt down to watch them make their pictographs. One fat copyist blew his nose and drew a red circle around a word-picture.

"This is the name of a king," he told her, as he drew an umbrella. "The crown of Northern Egypt is red, of the South, white. And the Pharoah is the son of Ra, the Sun God."

He drew a duck and put a dot inside. This was the ideograph for the word sun. He stood up to go and have a glass of water.

"There are Forty-two Commandments in *The Book of the Dead,*" Thoth told her. Thank God, Moses only gave us ten when he went out of this country, thought Padma.

"The Book also contains the histories of twenty dynasties which ruled over Egypt during the last three thousand years," Thoth further explained. This dancer from abroad didn't seem to know anything about the Glory That Was Egypt.

"Your Highness," one cheeky scribe cut him short— "Lemme go. My house is very far. And wife is sick. Can you give me yesterday's wages?"

"I've paid you already. You have even taken next week's advance," Thoth replied indignantly.

"Sir, give me some advance, too. My son is not well. The prices are going up and up because of the war—" another scribe whined.

Ah, the romance of Land of the Pharoas—Padma strolled down to the end of the corridor. After he had dealt with the unruly scribes, Thoth joined her again. He had brought a scroll with him.

"This is a hymn from the *Book of the Dead*. It may interest you," he said in order to entertain her, for she looked bored. "Listen—" he leaned against the balustrade and began reading out— "It is titled— A dead man comes to life and praises the Sun God Ra—.

"As thou rose in Thy radiant glory Thy priests came out laughing. Thy Boat of the Dawn came alongside the Barge of Night. And Annu's halls resounded with voices. Ages shall pass. Time shall keep blowing up its dust under Thee, Thou that art yesterday and today and tomorrow, O Ra! Millions of years have passed, millions— Anuti get the dinner ready—" he said in the same breath.

The hymn had reminded her of *The Rock of Ages*. "You have an early dinner," she remarked.

"Yeah, mosquitoes and moths become a nuisance after sundown."

"What are you doing in the evening?"

"Anuti—" he shouted again. "Find out the time of *The Eye of Horus.*"

"It has started already," she replied tartly. She was quite cheeky, too. It seemed that his staff took advantage of his good nature.

"All right. Dinner can wait." He addressed Padma disinterestedly, "Let me take you out. I have seen this play so many times that it bores me to tears. You may like it."

A lot of fashionable people were going towards the theatre hall. Heliopolis was a vast locality. Thoth and Padma kept walking till they came to a tiny pyramid. A crowd was assembled in the adjacent temple.

"What's happening here?" asked Padma.

"They must be paying homage to the soul of some departed king. Would you like to see?" He held her hand and took her inside the congested courtyard of the temple.

"Whose anniversary?" Thoth asked someone.

"The Pharoah Nafrka Ra—," came the reply. In the stone basement of the tomb the late Pharoah's open coffin stood upright against the granite walls. His mummy looked very life-like. It was tied up in Indian muslin.

"He died quite recently— only about a thousand years ago," Thoth whispered to Padma.

The priest's frightening incantation rose above the murmur of the congregation, "O King Nafr-Ka-Ra, accept the Eye of Horus and take it to thy face." Then he placed a piece of bread and a golden cup full of beer on a tray and presented it to the mummy.

"O Nafr-Ka-Ra, whose glory and might have vanished, look upon what has come from there, and take your bath. Through the grace of Horus, open thy mouth, O King—"

Padma felt suffocated in the crowd of worshippers. Thoth noticed her discomfort and led her out. "Now, would you care to see the play?"

"That, too, would have this Eye of Horus business? Well, I have come so far on foot, I may as well see it," she said resignedly.

Thoth brought her back to the main street. Poor thing. He is doing his best trying to entertain me. But how else shall I spend this dark and depressing evening?

The play[1] was in progress. The gods Horus, Thoth, Seth, Osiris, and a few milkmaids, butchers and children were strutting about on the stage. Said "Horus" to the kids—"Fill the world with my Eye—" The curtain came down, went up and the second scene began— A necklace of agate was brought on the stage. Said "Horus" to "Seth"— I have picked up my Eye which is like agate for thee. Bring my Eye which became blood-red when it went into thy mouth—"

"What's all this about?" Padma whispered to her host.

"Seth the God of Storms had blinded Horus, the God of Bright Blue Sky. He returns the Eye to Horus—which means— pleasant weather follows the time of strong gales."

Oh, Padma thought: Dust storms have been blinding the Egyptians down the ages. In ancient times they made the calamity a part of their mythology.

"This play would continue till midnight. The moon has risen. Would you like to go boating on the Nile?"

"Thoth, if you don't mind, I would rather go home, have some dinner and get some sleep. I have to be in my office at eight in the morning. . . " Suddenly she checked herself again. Luckily Thoth hadn't heard her because he was busy clearing the way for her through the aisle.

Back in his house she asked him at the dinner table, "Thoth, why did you think I was spying for the Hebrews, I mean, the Aprus? Are these people a problem for you?"

"Yes," he replied, taking out a bone from fried fish. The torches, light flickered over his handsome, thoughtful face. "But our rulers have solved the Hebrew Question in an extremely inhuman manner. All the able-bodied men of that race have to work as serfs. Many of these Pyramids have been built by Apru slave gangs. They carry tons of stone on their bare backs and die young, spitting blood. Poor Mikhael is an old friend of mine. He had got a job as a clerk in the River Customs. He thought he would be saved this fate. But his name has been included in the

---

1. This play was first staged on the occasion of the coronation of Pharoah Sioprus I. French archeologists found its Ms in Ras Shamari.

new list."

"You can't do anything about it?"

"How can one person fight against the Establishment? Our entire system has become rotten."

Dinner over, he took her upstairs, to a large bedroom. Its floor was made of yellow Sudanese stone and furnished with an ornate fourposter, a centre table of mahagony and a chair. The dressing table had a mirror made of shining steel. A bejewelled comb, a fish-shaped container for kohl; powder and rouge were kept inside jars studded with semi-precious stones.

"This is my younger sister's bedroom. As I told you, she is away in Thebes. You sleep here in comfort and get up in the morning, whenever you like. If you need anything just call Anuti. She will sleep in the corridor. Good night."

"Good night, Thoth."

Padma sat down on the bed and looked out of the window. There was a red-stone tank full of pink lotuses down below. It was the night of the full moon. The desert breeze was cool and refreshing. After a little while, she fell asleep.

A big African mosquito stung her nose. Vastly irritated, she got up and resumed looking out of the window.

Heptatonic notes of flute rose in the stillness of the night. She peeped down. Thoth sat by the tank, playing his reed-pipe.

So help me God. Has the poor boy fallen in love with me? Sitting there playing the flute at midnight like an idiot. I must run away from here—first thing in the morning. I remember the way from Heliopolis to the city gate. From there I can reach my rocket in half an hour. I'll get home by 7 a.m. Fortunately her brothers had gone to Cochin for a few days and nobody would know where she had spent the night. The part-time maid came at 9 a.m..

Listening to her host's haunting melody, she dozed off again.

A resounding voice woke her up at five in the morning. She raised her head from the pillow and watched a man of imposing height, standing by the tank. He faced the rising sun and waved his arms and declaimed, "Hail to thee, O Ra, Hail Aton, Hail Kharpar— Welcome O Eye of Horus— Aton—Sun God—The greatest creator, Tah—Tah who resides in the hearts of all living beings. Whatever he thinks happens. He created the universe with his word[1]. Tah Tanin—Khapri riding the Barge—Aton—Creator of adjinns and human beings, giver of food, who differentiated the nations of the world through the colours of their skins. The Nile flows through his love. Merciful, compassionate— one God— alive, who keeps alive the fish of the river and the birds of the sky. Who sustains insects and flies. Amon— Amon Harakhite, keep shining over me— there is no God but Thee—"

Ra's rays began to spread over the horizon. The priest strode back to Thoth's family temple, which could be seen through the early morning mist. Padma took out her wristwatch from her bag. She had had no coffee or tea since yesterday and therefore had a severe headache. What do these folks have for breakfast, she wondered. It's amazing— how did people manage before the discovery of tea and coffee? Now look at Thoth. He is living so happily. No coffee. No cigarette. No cinema, or telephone, TV, airplanes, advertising, public relations, journalism. . . Poor guy. He is not aware of any of these things.

Plop—she peeped down again. Mr Thoth Junior had dived in the pool and the reflection of its blue waters was dancing like mermaids upon the palace's outer walls of yellow stone.

Thoth began swimming, looked up at Padma's window, and got busy plucking a red lotus—obviously to present to her.

Run—run—must get the hell out of here—at once— she got up frantically, put on her chappals, and opened the bedroom door. All male and female slaves were snoring away in the galleries. She went downstairs and ran past the huge statue of Ipis, the holy bull.

She came out in the street. The door of the houses on either side were still closed. A few vegetable sellers and fishmongers had appeared and could be seen moving about in the mist. She reached the city gate, and found it

---

1.   Ain-ul-Shams in Arabic. There is an Ainul Shams University in modern Cairo.
2.   This hymn was written in 3400 B.C. "In the beginning was the Word——" The opening lines of the Gospel according to St. John was written in the early Christian era.

locked. One of its sentries challenged her—Halt, O wench—
where art thou going?

"To the river—," she faltered. "I am a fishwife."

"You are a very foolish fishwife, in that case. Don't you
know that His Majesty is coming back from the war-front?
The gate won't be opened before his arrival."

"When will he come?"

"Donno, who the hell are you to ask?"

She felt weak and sat down on a wayside stone. She
badly needed a cup of hot coffee. Her headache had got
worse. The horrid Pharoah must be coming in his chariot
on snail's pace—God damn him. How long would he take
in reaching this blasted gate? And by this time that bitch
Anuti must have told Thoth that the Indian dancer has
run away. What would he think about me? I shouldn't
have absconded like this. Now he may really believe that
I am an Assyrian spy, he may get me arrested, cast me in
a dungeon—Holy Mary, Mother of God. After years she
found herself fervently praying to Virgin Mary. Then she
realised that she was loudly repeating *Mother of God,
Mother of God* in the ancient Egyptian language. A sentry
came closer, and asked sternly, "Woman—art thou a slave-
girl of the temple of the Mother of God Horus—?"

Padma nodded helplessly.

"Brother Khofu—" the other sentry said, staring at her,
"this is the same sky-maiden a goatherd told me about
last night."

At once both bent down in a gesture of obeissance
before her. Right then the heavy padlock of the gate was
removed. The noise of pipes and drums rent the sky. Foot
soldiers, the cavalry, and the chariots of Government
officials came in view. Then followed the golden chariot of
the Pharoah. He wore an inordinately tall crown which
indicated that he was the King of both Northern and
Southern Egypt. He was a wrinkled old man, and looked
quite stupid. He sat erect with great aplomb as behove
such a mighty monarch. Padma tried to sneak away
through the massive throngs. A soldier barred her way
with his spear.

"The messenger of Goddess Hathor— The sky virgin,
Hail, Hail, Eye of Horus—" A tremendous din rose.

Surrounded by an over-enthusiastic crowd she felt suffocated and passed out.

When Dr. Padma Mary Abraham Kurian came to, she found herself lying on a coach in the private temple of the Royal Palace. Joss sticks were being lighted. A party of priests was repeating—Amon—Ra— Tah[1]—Tah—Tahyap— Nobody knows what is going to happen. Or when would God give his verdict. Serapis—Edfu—Tah—Tah—Tah—

Dr. Kurian felt dizzy and collapsed once again. The lecherous old Pharoah was sitting on his golden chair ogling her. A kindly gentleman who resembled Thoth Junior, and was probably senior Thoth, sat on a stool.

The gigantic Chief Priest and some temple maidens helped Padma sit up.

She said weakly—and in English, "Thank you— Black coffee please, no sugar—"

The Pharoah was trembling with fear. "What does the sky-maiden say?" he asked the Chief Priest.

The Priest quaked: "Your Majesty, I am sorry I cannot understand this heavenly language."

The Pharoah stood up, folded his hands and addressed Dr. Kurian:

"O Venus, O daughter of the High Heavens! It is our great good fortune that right during the critical days of our war against Assyria the Mother of God has sent you down as her emissary and this surely augers well for us. We are going to be victorious. Since I am the earthly son of Ra, as a gesture of thanksgiving to the Queen of Heaven I shall marry you at five o'clock sharp according to Memphis Standard Sundial Time."

Padma opened her eyes wide and looked at him in horror. This dreadful man, whose mummy I have seen in the British Museum— I am to marry him tomorrow! She felt giddy again and closed her eyes.

"The celestial lady had gone into deep meditation," the Chief Priest whispered. There was tense, respectful silence in the room. At that moment Padma thought of a strategy and saw the glint of a vague and dim hope.

She opened her eyes and said feebly, "I want to be left alone. I must commune with the Mother of God—"

---

1. Ancient Egyptian Trinity. Tah was supposed to have eight incarnations, not unlike the Indian avatars.

The Pharoah and his cronies at once rose to their feet. Padma relayed another message from On High, "Before my nuptials, keep all doors open, remove all sentries. I am expecting an angel or two from above."

"As you wish, O daughter of Tah," the head priest bowed deeply.

"Any earthly creature— man, woman, child, bird, beast— must not show me their faces."

All of them, including the King, vanished. Padma had not eaten since the morning. She polished off the consecrated fruit and sweets which had been given to her as offering. Then she helped herself to the consecrated sherbet. Feeling a little better, she got up and looked out of the trellised balcony. Torches were being lit. Musicians were carrying their wind and string instruments towards the Banquet Hall. Preparations were afoot for the royal wedding. Gradually all became quiet. After a while a pair of Hebrew slaves went past the balcony, whispering, "The old fogey has gone bonkers— marrying this girl, whoever she is . . . I don't believe she has come down from the Heavens."

After half an hour Padma tiptoed out. At the end of the passage an old Hebrew slave stood erect, holding a torch. Padma was overjoyed. She beckoned to him. He placed the torch in the wall-bracket and came towards her. Padma said in his ears, "Uncle, I am no sky maiden sent by their imaginary goddess. . . ."

The old man looked at her intently. Hardships had made him very cautious. He remained silent. Padma whispered again, "My name is Mirium bint Ibrahim. I swear upon the God of Ibrahim and Isaac, I am no heathen."

The persecuted Hebrews immediately recognised one another. This women did not look one of them. Her facial features were very different. But she had sworn upon the God of Abraham. The old man was worried.

"Rabbi—" Padma said earnestly, "do you also believe that I am the so-called goddess Hothor's emissary?"

"Nonsense!" the old Hebrew blurted out.

"I am Mirium bint Ibrahim."

"Praise be to the One True God."

"Please somehow take me to the house of Mikhael bin

Hannan—"

"That's a very common name. Give me some more details."

"He works with the River Customs—and knows Prince Thoth—"

"Prince Thoth at this moment is dining and wining with the accused Pharoah in the palace. What do you have to do with that idolator, O Mirium bint Ibrahim?"

"Nothing. Nothing at all, uncle."

"Follow me." He took off his black cloak and she covered herself in it from head to toe. He extinguished the torch and took her out of a secret door. Passing through dark lanes and by-lanes they reached the ghetto. The old man knocked at a door.

"Shalom Aleikum, O Yaqoob bin Shamoon."

"Shalom. Who are you?"

"Hazqeel bin Zakaria."

"Come in."

It was a Friday evening. An old Hebrew and his family sat around a lighted manorah and sang a hymn in melody Adatoon.

Padma Mary took off her cloak and sat down on a mat. Mikhael bin Hannan came out of the adjoining room. Hizqueel said something in his ear and he went out.

That Friday evening of the spring of 1315 B.C. (this writer does not know the name of the ancient Egyptian calendar's month and date) Mary Kurian told them her story and heard their tale of woes. They were present in her very remote past. And she had come to them from their extremely distant future. But these extraordinarily intelligent people readily understood what she told them, especially young Mikhael bin Hannan who grilled her with questions. The Yaqoob bin Shamoon said slowly, "Our forefather was an Aramaic—Ibrahim—who lived beyond the river Euphrates—Ibr-un-Nehr, that's why we came to be called Ibrani, people from beyond the river. He lived in the Chaldean city of Ur. He took his family along and came out of the valley of the Euphrates, and went about looking for pastures in the days of famine. Canaan—Egypt—Canaan again—Then Yaqoob bin Ishaq bin Ibrahim had twelve sons—and Yusuf bin Yaqoob—"

"Yes, yes. I know all that," Padma interrupted him impatiently. The night was passing. If Mikhael could take her by boat to the place where the rocket was parked—
"Yusuf was sold in the marketplace of Memphis. But God was with him." the old man continued.

"Yes, yes," Padma cut him short again. "Joseph—I mean, Yusuf, was eventually made Egypt's Minister of Food and Agriculture and he sent for his clan from Canaan."

"And Beni Israel multiplied and flourished in Egypt. A new Pharoah grew afraid that they would become powerful and must be curbed. So they were turned into slave labour and they were made to build cities for their Egyptian overlords."

"Yes. And then the Pharoah told the Hebrew sages to kill all the newborn male babies of their community—" Padma could not help quoting from the Second Book of Old Testament.

Her hosts were taken aback. "What are you saying? When did this happen?"

Then she decided she must tell them that the day of their deliverance was about to dawn. She went to the window and saw the lights of the Royal Palace glittering in the distance. She continued, "And then King Ramases II will order the Hebrews to drown all their newborn boys in the river."

"Are we going to have more troubles?" her hostess asked anxiously.

"Yes, indeed. But one baby called Moshe will survive and he will be brought up right there in the Palace of Ramases II and he will take you all out of Egypt"

The Hebrews looked at her in amazement. "Girl! Are you a sorceress? Or an oracle?"

"Well, you may say that I happen to know about the future. Then you, Beni Israel, will found a kingdom in Canaan. And the King of Assyria will conquer you and take you in captivity to Babylon, where you will write the Torah. And Cyrus, the Emperor of Persia, will liberate you and send you back to Palestine. And over there Jesus will be born in the House of King David." Unconsciously she made the sign of the cross. The Hebrews gazed at her, spellbound. She continued, "And then, the Romans will

deport you and you will be called the Wandering Jews.
And, after more than three thousand years from now, in
the 1948th year after the birth of Jesus, you will exile the
Arabs from their land, just as other nations had exiled you
and on for two thousand years in Europe, and you will set
up the state of Israel."

"Who are the Arabs?" the host asked.

Padma was exhausted. She told them very briefly about
the international situation of her own time.

Mikhael was listening to her in rapt attention. He said,
"Your science has progressed so much that you have
flown faster than the speed of light and returned to the
past. What next?"

Dawn was breaking over the Nile.

"I don't know, Mikhael. Please take me quickly to my
rocket."

"Take us with you forward to your own time," the
Hebrews implored.

"No," Padma said, firmly, "my heart bleeds for you, but
we can't go ahead or behind our own era. We are destined
to bear the hardships and misfortunes of our epochs. We
cannot shift history back and forth. I am telling you all
this like Deborah of Israel, who will be born in your
society after a few centuries. However, I have come from
the age of scientists, not of prophets."

The Hebrews began to shed tears. Young Mikhael had
hardened his face and learned stoically against the brick
well. Padma looked at him sadly. There was a knock at
the door. They became alert. Yaqoob's wife hid Padma
under a blanket. Mikhael opened the door.

Prince Thoth stood in the threshold.

The kindly prince told the Hebrews to extinguish the
lamps, and turned to Padma. "I was attending the royal
banquet, when one of my slaves came in and told me on
the quiet that the sky-maiden had disappeared. A sentry
had seen you going towards the ghetto. I told the slave to
hold his tongue and have come here straight.

"You didn't tell me in the morning and ran away. You
have landed yourself in a terrible mess. The Pharoah is
hellbent on making you his queen. Right now he and his
courtiers and generals are all lying under the table. But as
soon they get up they will catch you and if they suspect

that you are an Assyrian spy they will tie you to a stone and drown you in the Nile. I may be able to save you if you tell me the truth about yourself. Who on earth are you?"

Padma and the Hebrews looked at one another helplessly. She thought, the Hebrews are my spiritual ancestors. They have reached the stage of spiritual and intellectual evolution that they could comprehend what I told them about myself. But would this poor blighter, Thoth, who worships dead cats and idols of gods with faces of dogs and bulls—would he be able to grasp my reality?

"Mirium, tell him," Mikhael whispered to her, "or he may also take you to be a foreign spy or a sorceress, and then he would certainly hand you over to the authorities."

Briefly, Padma told him. She was flabbergasted when she realised that Thoth, too, understood about her. He remained silent and then said, "Well, we know mathematics and astronomy. And nobody has yet been able to solve this business of Time and Eternity. As far as I gather, nor have you, in your age. And since we Egyptians cannot solve the mystery of Time we are so preoccupied with mummies. Anyway, come along, I'll take you to your time-machine."

When she said goodbye to the Hebrews, they started weeping bitterly. Their race was going to produce Moses, and Jesus, and Karl Marx, and Sigmund Freud, and Einstein. However, at that moment in the darkness of 1315 B.C., Padma left them behind in utter despair. That's the reason man has not been given the faculty of foreseeing the future or look back at the past, or else we, too, would die weeping.

When Padma reached the date palms on Thoth's swift chariot, the rocket glimmered in the rays of Ra— (she had already started thinking like the ancient Egyptians!). Padma said a hearty Thank the Lord! *And though I walk in the Valley of The Shadow of Death, I fear no evil—* she muttered the psalm. Before she could finish her relieved, tearful thanksgiving, she saw a cloud of dust rising on the side of the city gate. Some horsemen were rushing down towards her, shining their spears. Padma quickly climbed the rocket's stair. The door opened. She got in. Thoth was standing outside. He screamed, "Take me along. They would kill me. They would kill me for letting you escape, help me, I have saved your life. Now you save mine."

Nervously Padma pulled him in by his hand. The door closed. she pressed the button marked 1966 A.D.

The rocket landed on the lawn of Dr. Kurian's cottage behind the palm grove. It was early morning. All was quiet. There was nobody around. Padma pushed the rocket inside the motor garage and locked the gate. Thoth seemed utterly bewildered as he glanced around. He looked so funny in his gold-and-black sarong, and fringe cut. His massive necklace of gold sparkled in the early morning sun. Padma's heart sank. What would the poor fellow do in this present-day world? She led him inside. Her brothers wouldn't return from Cochin till the Easter Holidays were over. The maid would come at nine. She took Thoth to the boys' room and opened their wardrobe. She managed to find some clothes which could fit him.

"Take a shower and change. I'll take you to the tailor's shop in the afternoon," she said and went into the dining room. She opened the fridge, took out eggs and butter, made toast on her toaster, prepared coffee in the perculator. Then she picked up *The Times of India* from the verandah, scanned its headlines and switched on the stove to boil eggs.

"Hi! good morning!"

She looked up, startled. Thoth stood in the door grinning away to glory, smoking her brother John's cigarette. He asked in an American accent, "Breakfast ready?" Then he sat down and began reading *The Times of India.*

Kindly note that just as Padma had started understanding, speaking and reading the ancient Egyptian and Semitic languages as soon as she had landed in 1315 B.C., immediately, on his arrival in A.D. 1966., Thoth Junior had acquired the knowledge of English, Malayalam and Hindi.

To cut a long story short, as they say, Padma introduced him to her colleagues and friends as a Coptic Christian friend from Egypt who was an artist by profession and specialised in painting frescos and pictures in the ancient

Egyptian style. She had met him in the States where he had been teaching Egyptian Culture at a university.

The ancient art of Egypt has been as thoroughly commercialised by modern Egypt just as we have commercialised our Ajanta paintings. Al-Syed Dr. Thoth-al-Hermez made a few paintings which were sold immediately. He shifted to Bombay and rented a small flat on Cumballa Hill. Soon he became a popular and affluent member of the city's fashionable society. Somehow he managed to acquire the passport of a Gulf state, and frequently visited Europe and America. More handsome than Omar Sharif, and a professional charmer, Thoth was having the time of his life.

Many year passed. Padma continued to slog in her Space Research Lab in the South. One day her mother asked her, "This Coptic Christian friend of yours—is he not interested in marriage?"

Padma kept quiet. Thoth had no time for her. He hardly met her though regularly sent her Christmas and New Year cards. The fact of the matter was that poor Padma was a plain Jane, and the glamorous Mons. Hermez had become a celebrity, surrounded by the most beautiful fashion models and starlets of Bombay. And the other undeniable fact was that a man may belong to 1315 B.C. or A.D. 1966, he would remain the same—unreliable.

In June, 1975, Padma came to Bombay on two weeks' leave to visit an ailing aunt who lived in Bandra. One evening she rang Thoth up and invited him for dinner at her aunt's place.

"Why don't you come over?" he sounded bored and listness. "Bandra is too far from here. They impounded my licence for rash driving and I hate Bombay taxis."

Padma realised that he had become too big for his boots. Still, she considered him her responsibility and was a little worried about the tiredness in his voice. She took a cab and reached his luxury apartment on Cumballa Hill.

He sat before his TV set, brooding. A discussion was going on about Egypt and Israel. Padma sat down on a sofa chair. He switched off the television and turned towards her.

"I want to go right back to Egypt and fight," he declared sombrely.

"Your Kippur War was waged nearly a decade ago," Padma replied.

"Ramadhan War—" he corrected her sternly.

"O.K. Ramazan War."

"I'll enlist in the Egyptian Army."

"For that you are probably over-age, dear Thoth."

"Keep quiet!" he growled and filled another glass of whiskey.

"You have started drinking too much."

"Don't talk to me like a nagging wife."

"I beg your pardon!" Padma flared up.

"Sorry, Padma, I'm sorry," he said softly. He looked very unhappy.

"Thoth, dear, what's the matter?" Padma asked with concern. "Going back to Egypt is no problem. You can take the next Air India flight to Cairo."

"No, shall I tell you?" he said after a pause. "I wish to return to my own time."

"To your own time?" Padma repeated, astonished. "You want to leave this day and age?"

"What's so great about this day and age? What's the big deal?" He switched on the television again. The newsreal was showing scene after scene of wars, religious, and racial, and political, bloodshed, taking place all over the world.

"Tell me how much more civilised have you become after more than three thousand years? We persecuted the Israelites and we fought against the Assyrians and others. You all live in perfect peace and total harmony, and adore one another. Our pharoahs were cruel despots. Your rulers are angelic. We were scared of death. You have liberated yourselves from the fear of extinction. You do not build magnificent tombs. You do not venerate the deceased. You do not write elegies and books of the dead. You have also given up writing poetry. We worshipped strange deities. Your religions are utterly rational." He put his glass on the table and laughed derisively. "Your wars are based on humanism. Your nuclear bomb is a symbol of your love for mankind. The speed of your light is very, very fast indeed."

"Thoth, you are merely feeling out of time and disoriented, momentarily. That's all. Let's go to a movie."

"Blast the movies and leave me alone."

"O.K." She rose to her feet and advanced towards the door. "Good night, Thoth."

"Padma," he called out, "I apologise for my outburst. Padma—"

"It's all right, Thoth."

"Padma. Come here. Sit down. Listen. The thing is that I am missing my parents and my sisters. I want to go home. That rocket of yours, is it still locked up in your garage?"

"Yes. But I feel terribly scared. I don't even want to think about it, and nobody knows about my secret."

"Fly me back to the Remote Past. I have seen enough of the Future."

"You are not being fair, Thoth. We are not so bad really. You merely have a bout of depression, that's all."

"Maybe. But I am feeling acutely homesick—"

"Time-sick," she corrected him. "O.K., as you wish. But remember. I have studied the rocket's manual which I found later. It was placed under the pilot's seat. This space-time ship can fly only four times, faster than the speed of light, after which it will explode. When I take you back to Memphis, and come back, I won't be able to return to your time and fetch you back to the present."

"Agreed," he said happily.

1306 B.C. The goatherd was still there, playing his flute by the pond. He had grown up in the intervening nine years. The moment he saw Padma and Thoth coming out of the rocket he prostrated in obeisance. Before leaving A.D. 1975 Thoth had put on his Egyptian dress, and had become the same old Prince Thoth once again.

"I won't go to town. Your Pharoah would again get hold of me," said Padma.

"Is His Majesty in residence in Memphis or has gone to Thebes?" Thoth asked the herdsman.

"The last Pharoah is dead, Your Highness." He pointed towards the horizon where a new pyramid was under construction. "Rameses II is now the King. And he is at the moment in Thebes, Sire."

"Come along, Padma. I'll take you to Thebes. Stay there for a while and then go back to A.D. 1975 This new Pharoah is a nice chap. He is my childhood friend. He won't even think of marrying you. He is madly in love with his queen. Come along."

They hired a barge to sail up to Thebes. Thoth looked immensely happy and relieved, back in antiquity.

It was a long voyage on the Nile. They passed by Hearadeopolis and continued sailing for a few days.

Magnificent temples and palaces appeared over the horizon.

"They have all been submerged in the Aswan Dam." Thoth remarked indignantly.

"No, many have been removed and saved," she tried to pacify him.

The barge passed by the colossal statues of kings and queens. They landed at the grand staircase of the summer palace. Thoth's parents, sisters and other members of the royal family sat in a verandah on armchairs, enjoying the river scene. It was a languid summer evening and the sun was slowly going down in the waters of the Nile. Thoth told his family that the Goddess Hathor had ordered him not to disclose where he had been all this time when the Celestial Maiden took him away on her flying carriage, nine years ago.

Padma enjoyed herself in the summer palace and looked around slyly to see if Baby Moses was lying in some cradle in the royal nursery. She was disappointed. On the fourth day she bade adieu to her highly sophisticated, elegant hosts, left Thebes. Thoth accompanied her to the date-palm grove to see her off.

Padma was struck dumb. The rocket was not there. Her legs shivered. She felt the earth slipping from under her feet. She sat down weekly on the sand. Thoth was horrified too. He called peasants. They searched far and wide and could not find the rocket. He returned to Padma who sat with her head between her knees. Then he caught a glimpse of a piece of yellow papyrus which had been placed under a stone. He pulled it out. It was the usual identity slip of a Hebrew slave with his name and number inscribed on it. On the other side there was a letter written in blood. Being a trained librarian, Thoth read the Sinai script at a glance and turned pale. With trembling hands he gave it to Padma. Once again she understood an ancient language—in which the blood—curdling message was written from right to left.

Mirium bin Ibrahim—Shalom Aleichem. Today while I was carrying stones for the pyramid which is being built for the late Pharoah, the slave-driver whipped me so hard that I fainted. When I regained consciousness I managed to drag myself here to drink some water from the pond. And I saw your rocket gleaming like an angel of mercy. I remember every word of what you had told me that dark night in our ghetto nine years ago. During the last three days I had overheard the Egyptian architects at the construction site saying to one another that the sky-maiden had brought back Prince Thoth from On High and had gone to Thebes. So I think that you would stay here as a royal guest for some time. They won't let you go back in a hurry.

I have dipped a reed in the blood still oozing out of my wounds, to write to you. You had told us that Moshe would be born in the reign of Ramases II. And for all you know, while I am penning these lines, he may have already been born in one of the homes of our ghetto. But it will take him some years to grow up. I can't wait for the Exodus. Now, if I return to the building site, the Chief Slaves-driver is so angry with me, he may bury me alive in the sand. Therefore, to save my dear life I am taking off in your rocket and zoom into your time. First, I'll go to New York about which you had told me that night. After that, Israel. And I swear upon the God of Abraham and Isaac, that as soon as I get settled there, I'll come here in this very rocket, and take you back to your time which from the next minute is my time too.

Your brother-in-faith
Mikhael bin Hannan bin Yaqoob,
(from today Michael H. Jacob alias Mike).

Padma collapsed on the sand. Thoth sprinkled some water over her fade. When she came to, he tried to re-assure her, "Padma dear, he has promised to return and take you back to A.D. 1975 I have known him for a long time. He is an honest and truthful young man. He will not let you down. Remember, in order to save my skin, I, too, had fled with you in your rocket. He will certainly bring your time-ship back."

"Thoth," Padma replied slowly, "before leaving A.D. 1975 I had told you that this faster-than-the-speed-of-light time-machine can fly only four times back and forth, after which it will blow up. Mikhael has gone away on its fourth and final trip."

6

A Night on Pali Hill

(All characters are entirely fictitious and bear no resemblance to any person living or dead.)

Homai Junkwalla
Rodaba Junkwalla
Aunt Feroza
Dara Kazimsadeh
Gulcher Isfandiari
Pali Hill, Bombay. An evening of July 1976.

A seedy old drawing-cum-dining room. Window in the middle of the back wall. Carved Goan furniture. Chinese vases. A camphor box. A sofa, three chairs and a cottage piano near the window. Oval-shaped gilt-framed portrait of an old, distinguished-looking Parsi couple, above the sofa. Large photograph of a handsome, smiling young man, on top of the piano next to the model of a Chinese junk. Right of the window a dining table laid for three, a couple of chairs. Toby mug, curious, photographs of Queen Elizabeth II and the Shah and Shahbanu of Iran on a sideboard, a cuckoo clock above the window. Homai, a middle-aged woman, clad in a black kimono is standing in the window, her back to the audience. Her younger sister Rodaba is playing "On Richmond Hill There Lived A Lass".

Homai: *(Harshly)* Don't disturb me, Rudy. I am trying to pray. *(Rodaba starts playing "It's The Last Rose of Summer Left Blooming Alone.")*

Homai: Rudy, it's the night of the Full Moon and I would like to recite my Mah Yanaish . . . There is going to be a downpour. How would poor Hoshang come? *(Rodaba* *continues to play. Outside it starts raining. Flash of lightning. Somebody starts tapping the roof. Off-stage cats howl. Sounds of thunderstorm.)*

Homai: *(loudly chanting the 101 Names of God)* Yazd . . . Harvasptwan Harvasp Agah. . . Harvasp Khoda Afza . . . Parwara .. Kharoshedta . . . Haryamd . . . Harnek Farah.. Farmankam. Afarmosh . . . Afrazdam . . . Adarbadgard.

Rodaba: *(Begins playing "The Old Kentucky Home", tilts her head back and sings)* Weep no more, my lady, O weep no more today, we shall sing one song of the old Kentucky Home, of the old Kentucky home far away . . .

Homai: *(Blocking her ears with her fingers, recites in a louder monotone)* Adarnamgar . . . Badnamgar . . . Badigulgar . . . Aguman . . . Azman . . . Ferozegar . . . Dadar . . . Natyafird Khradmand . . . Dawar . . .·
(There is a loud knock on the door).

Rodaba: *(Swings round on her stool)* Somebody has come!
(The call bell rings)
(Homai goes to the door, opens it cautiously, peeps out, turns towards Rodaba)

Homai: Young foreigners!

Rodaba: Hippies?

Homai: No. They look like a high-class English couple.
(Opens the door, a young man and a girl enter hesitatingly.)

Young Man: *(In an Oxford accent)* Thank you, Ma'am. Most kind of you. *(Helps the pretty blonde take off her raincoat. She is holding a parcel. They look like wealthy tourists.)*

Girl: *(In an American accent)* Do excuse us for barging in like this. We have been trying to find Mrs. Kulsum Zariwalla's house. It seems impossible to locate it in such weather. Maybe you could tell us. It is supposed to be in this neighourhood. *(Shows a slip of paper to Homai who remains silent, peering at the newcomers in wonder, as if they have stepped out of a long-ago beautiful dream. Rodaba crosses over and smiles* *reassuringly, takes the address from the girl, puts on her glasses and reads)*

Girl: The cabbie said this was Palimala Road.

Rodaba: No.

Young Man: Ma'am, the taxi driver refused to go further in this rain. May we stay here till the storm passes?

Homai: *(Suddenly as though waking up from her dream)*, Of course, of course, you are most welcome. Do come in and make yourself comfortable. I'll get you some hot tea.
(The handsome young pair look at each other with a slight hint of hesitation, come to the centre of the stage.)

Girl: Gee. Thanks *(Looks around).* What a cosy living room!

Homai: American?

Girl: No, Ma'am . . . Iranian.

Young Man: *(Introducing themselves with enormous courtesy)* Khanom Golchehr Isfandiari . . . Dara Kazemzadeh.

Homai & Rodaba: Pleased to meet you.
(The pair sit down on the sofa. Golchehr's locket with a diamond studded "Ya Ali' lights up as she faces the audience.
(Rodaba goes out briskly)

Homai: *(Sitting down on a chair)* Coming from England?

Dara: Yes, Ma'am. Last night, from London. I am studying at Oxford. Golchehr is at Sarah Lawrence, in the United States.

Gulchehr: An Indian classmate of mine, Khadija Zariwalla, had given a letter and a packet to be delivered to her mother, Mrs. Kulsum Zariwalla, over here on Pali Hill. So we came looking for the house.

Dara: Miss Zariwalla had also given the phone number of her mother's house. We telephoned from Hotel Centaur, but the lines were out of order because of the rains. *(Rodaba enters, carrying the teatray, places it on the centre table)* Gulchehr and I have come to see India, during our vacation. (*Noticing the keen interest on the old ladies' faces, he explains further*) We are first-cousins and also engaged to be married after we finish our studies. Before returning to the West, we'll go home to visit our parents.

Homai: Home?

Dara: Tehran . . . Iran.

Homai: Oh, of course.

(*Dara looks up and glances at the colour photograph of his King and Queen, Mohamed Reza Pehlavi and Farah Pehlavi, he is a bit surprised and pleased. Homai is very quiet. It seems as though she is entertaining guests after a very long time and does not quite know what to say to them.*)

Rodaba: (*More practical, pouring tea*) Homai dear, have you introduced ourselves to our charming guests? Young man! I am Rodaba Junkwalla and this is my elder sister, Miss Homai Junkwalla. (*Dara and his cousin nod and smile. Rodaba points at the portraits on the wall*) And our parents, Sir Ardeshir Kaikaous and Lady Junkwalla. (*Dara and Gulchehr look fascinated.*)

Rodaba: (*Pointing towards the photograph of the good-looking young man on the piano*) And that is Hoshang Saroshyar Mirza... Homai's fiance. (*Homai blushes like a young girl and coyly bends down her head. Dara and Gochehr look surprised. Somebody begins tapping the roof again. The young pair wince and look at each other. Rodaba offers them cups of tea*).

Dara: Thanks. How very nice of you.

Rodaba: Take a piece of cake. Homai baked it today. And I made the cottage cheese and scones.

Dara: Good Lord! Cottage cheese and scones! I feel as if I am still in England!

Homai: (*Dryly*) Young man, when you go out of this house you'll realise how standards have fallen. I do hope you are able to find Mrs. Pochkhanawalla's bungalow, if it hasn't already been pulled down to make way for some monstrous skyscraper. You said Mrs. Pochkhanawalla lives on. . .

Gulchehr: Mrs. Zariwalla.

Homai: Carter Road?

Golchehr: No, Palimala Road. The cabbie took us all over the Hill. Somebody in the hotel had told us that the place would be somewhere near Dilip Kumar's house. Then on the way a guy directed us to Rajesh Khanna's bungalow. I said to the cabbie, "Dilip Kumar and Rajesh Khanna's houses seem to be famous landmarks over here," and he said, "No, Madam, Meena Kumari used to live in 'Landmark' " *(giggles)*. Anyway, we did come up to Rajesh Khanna's house, then got lost.

Homai: *(Haughtily)* And who is Rajesh Khanna?

Rodaba: Homai dear, Rajesh Khanna is an Indian cinema actor. So is Dilip Kumar.

Golchehr: I have seen quite a few Indian movies in Tehran. My Mom saw *'Sangam'* thrice. She loved Vijayantimala and Raj Kapoor. Remember, Dara, when we were kids Indian movies used to be so popular in Tehran? And I still remember those two songs 'Dost dost na raha,' and 'Meri Jan shab bakher. . . *(turns to Rodaba)* Miss Junkwalla, do you know these songs?

Rodaba: *(firmly)* No. I do not.

Dara: *(puts down his cup of tea, crosses over to the window, looks out and turns to Golchehr)*. Golchehr, it has stopped raining. Let's take leave of our kind hostesses. *(The sisters look disappointed. He hesitates and looks around)* Ma'am, you have a lovely collection of Chinese curio!

Homai: *(Her face lights up with sudden pride)* My great-grandfather started trade with China. He had his own junks which sailed the China seas.

Dara: *(Genuinely)* Ah! Slow Boat to China and all that! How absolutely fascinating!

Homai: *(suddenly seems very keen to tell him all about herself)*. Before the Depression, most of the bungalows down this street belonged to our family. After the Crash they were all sold off. Our trade with China also came to an end.

Dara: Where are your parents?

Homai: *(Flatly)* They are dead.

Dara: Brothers?

Homai: *(in the same monotone)* They are also dead.

Dara: Any close relatives?

Homai: They are dead, too.

Dara: Oh, I'm sorry.

Homai: It is all right. What can you do about it. *(tap . . . tap . . . tap . . . on the roof)*

Golchehr: *(finishes her tea and looks at her cousin)* Dara. . .

Rodaba: *(Quickly)* No — No. Don't go away so soon. Have dinner with us.

Dara: Thank you, Ma'am. But its getting very late, and the taxi is waiting outside.

Rodaba: Send it away. Hoshang is about to arrive. He will take you to your hotel. Santa Cruz is not very far from here.

Homai: *(startled)* We have 1938 model Packard. I used to drive it myself. Poona for the weekends. Mahabaleshwar and Matheran during the summers. Can't drive now because of my arthritis. The motor car has been lying in the garage for the last 15 years. But let Hoshang come. I'll ask him to take you to your hotel in our Packard.

Dara: *(Quickly)* No—You mustn't bother. We'll go back in our cab.

Homai: *(resignedly)* All right. As you wish. My Hoshang also never wants to drive my poor old Packard. Comes and goes in a taxi.

Golchehr: *(Suddenly in a bored voice)* When will Mr. Hoshang come? *(The bird comes out of the cuckoo clock and whistles)*

Rodaba: He'll be here any moment. He is a bridge friend. Goes every evening to the Willingdon Club. Comes here around 9.30 or so. How long are you going to be in Bombay? We'll ask Hoshang to take you to the club one evening. Even today in this city taken over by upstarts the Willingdon Club retains its old elegance and British atmosphere . . .

Dara: *(Politely)* How interesting!

Golchehr: Sounds like the country clubs of New England!

Homai: You are so right! I visited America with my parents before the Depression. New York, Boston, Philadelphia, the Niagara Falls, everything. Even met Rudolph Valentino in Hollywood. He gave us his autographed photograph. I still have it somewhere. *(Enthusiastically)* Shall I show it to you? *(Stands up)*

Rodaba: *(Peeved)* Where will you hunt for it now? Forget about it.

Homai: *(Obediently)* All right. *(Sits down again, addressing Dara)* Rodaba and I went to a finishing school in Switzerland. My Hoshang went to Cambridge. . . like you . . .

Dara: *(Offended)* I am at Oxford.

Homai: *(Indifferently)* Never mind. Now I must go to the kitchen. Excuse me. *(Gets up and goes out of the door followed by Rodaba. Outside, the rain begins falling again. Roar of the sea. Flash of lightning. Dara returns to the window and looks out).*

Dara: *(Slowly)* My God! It's pitch dark outside. I have never seen such a dark night before. Night of the Indian Monsoons! The sea and the clouds and the night have all become one . . . (Gulchehr is growing frightened. She crosses over to Dara and stands close to him. He puts his arm around her protectively.)*

Gulchehr: Dara . . .

Dara: *(Peeping out)* Good Lord. Our taxi has vanished!

Gulchehr: *(Leans out of the window)* No, honey, it is right there, in the portico. But it's so dark. Not a single light downstairs. This delipidated mansion must have been quite imposing once. How strange! I have seen identical neo-Georgian houses on the cotton plantations in the Deep South.

Dara: *(Sadly)* Our hostesses are busy getting dinner for us.

Gulchehr: Delightful old ladies. Look like a pair of woodpeckers. Poor things.

Dara: *(Sadly)* Gulchehr. Never make fun of old age. Some day you and I shall also grow old. If we continue to live. . .

Gulchehr: *(Ashamed)* I am sorry, Dara.

Dara: *(Slowly, in a thoughtful voice)* Races grow old like individuals. An Indian Parsi friend of mine at Oxford told me that the entire population of the Parsis in the whole world was less than the circulation of *The Illustrated Weekly of India . . .!*

Gulchehr: Good God!

Dara: Remember, when we were coming down Malabar Hill today, the taxi driver pointed towards a wooded enclosure, and said that it was the famous Tower of Silence? And then it occurred to me—Pasardgard Persipolis, Ctesiphon. And in the end this! Lord, what an anti-climax.

Gulchehr: *(Ruefully)* Yes, it is very sad.

Dara: (In the some thoughtful voice) No. We need not feel sorry. We are still there. And these remarkable people, who created our ancient civilisation, shall also survive. Don't forget that they gave the world the concept of good and evil. *(The rain lets up. The window is lighted by a soft, milky white, rainwashed moonlight. Gradually, the light grows brighter.)*

Dara: Look Gulchehr. The Full Moon coming out of the dark clouds looks so magical, like a Constable landscape! Once this place must have been beautiful.

Gulchehr: The cabbie was telling us that only a decade ago Pali Hill was dotted with picturesque bungalows. Most of them have been pulled down and replaced by apartment blocks. *(After a pause)* Dara, I haven't come all the way from the States to see the so-called Skyscrapers of Bombay!

Dara: Gulchehr, we are leaving tomorrow for Jaipur, Agra, Delhi, Khajuraho—the works. We are sure to find the real India somewhere. Don't get bored so soon. *(It starts raining again. Enter Homai and Rodaba carrying* *trays full of covered dishes. They place the trays on the dining table and come back to their chairs. Dara and Gulchehr return to the sofa. Homai is very quiet, intently looking at her hands.)*

Dara: *(With genuine feeling)* Ma'am, both of you have such lovely, aristocratic hands . . . small and delicate— only meant for playing the piano and doing Retit print embroidery. *(The sisters look at him with grateful eyes.)*

Homai: *(Almost tearfully)* My dear young man. You are very kind. Very civilised. But our butler, housemaids, cook, left us long ago. For years we have been cooking and cleaning ourselves.

Dara: *(With sincerity)* You shouldn't have bothered about dinner for us. We could easily go back and eat at our hotel.

Homai: I shan't hear of it. Hoshang is about to come and we shall all dine together.

Dara: Very well. Thanks *(Gets up again and strolls around looking at the cracked Ming vases. Then she stops before the portraits, in oil, of Sir Ardeshir and Lady Junkwalla).*

Homai: *(Proudly)* Our parents *(wipes her eyes).*

Dara: (Softly) Yes. You told us *(sits down).*

Homai: *(In a flat, hoarse, matter-of-fact voice)* In the year 1934 when Papa went bankrupt, on a dark monsoon night like this, in this very room he wrapped a towel round his head and shot himself through his right temple.

Gulchehr (Shudders and moves closer to Dara)

Rodaba: Mama could not survive the grief and passed on after a few months. We were inconsolable. Our family Dastur told us, "Do not cry. According to the *Howdakht Naskh* God and His Prophet say that it is a sin to weep for the departed. Nobody, neither Balarawaneh Kaikaous who tried to fly to the Heavens, nor Afrsiab, Shah of Turan, who tried to hide from death in an iron palace beneath the sea, could escape extinction. When our parents passed on, all the sacred rites were duly performed and their mortal frames placed in the Tower.

For three nights a lamp burnt in our house. Do you know, if the Holy Avesta is not recited for the first three nights, the Angel Sarosh does not help the soul in the first stages of its journey onward. The first three nights are hard for the dead and seem like nine thousand nights. Drove after drove of demons try to frighten the soul in the Other World. But Sarosh helps a good soul across the Bridge. It is greeted by the Holy Ones and the angels and welcomed into Paradise—I am sure our Mama and Papa are in Paradise, (*wipes her tears*).

Dara: (*Gravely*) I am sure, Ma'am. (*Upstairs the tapping begins again. The Iranians are scared and look up.*)

Dara: (*Clearing his throat*) Ma'am. Do you have tenants upstairs? (*The sisters look at each other anxiously*)

Homai: (*To Rodaba*) Shall I tell them? (*Off-stage somebody is coming downstairs. An ancient Parsi lady enters through the right wing. She appears like an apparition— A high-necked blouse of white lace, white sari of china silk, worn in Parsi style, with a black beribboned velvet border, diamond brooch, diamond earrings. Rope of pearls round her throat. Gloves of white net, court shoes. It seems as though she is dressed for the Buckingham Palace garden party. Age about 95.*)

The Ancient Lady: (*In a rasping voice*) Homai, Rodaba— the Angel Sarosh helps nobody. Nor does Behram Yazd—nor Ahura Mazda Himself. Don't you delude yourself. Do you hear? All is Barzakh or Hell. There is no Paradise. Got it? I have come down at midnight to inform you that he has reached the Bridge and has faced Mehr Davar, and now my case is about to be presented before Mehr Yazd. 'Bye. (*She crosses the stage and goes out. Gulchehr clings to Dara in her fright. Rodaba and Homai are aghast. The clip-clop of the old lady going upstairs offstage. Silence*)

Rodaba: (*Recovers from the shock*) I'm sorry. This was our crazy aunt Feroza, former Lady Diamondcutter. She lives on the first floor. All by herself. She is 95 and batty, but look at her health and energy! Most of the time she keeps tapping the wooden floor of her bedroom with the point of her parasol, in order to annoy us. (*Dara and Gulchehr hold their hands tight.*)

Homai: (*Noticing their uneasiness*) I think before Hoshang arrives I may as well tell you the story of poor Aunt Feroza.

Rodaba: (*Sternly*) No. Homai, keep quiet.

Homai: No. I must tell them. (*The young couple stand up and move towards the exit. Homai grabs Dara's arm with extraordinary strength and pushes the boy and the girl towards the window.*) Do you see that burnt down mansion in front?

Dara: (*Stammers*) Yes—Yes—

Homai: This was Lady Feroza's house. (*Out of sheer habit Dara utters "How interesting," but checks himself.*) Aunt Feroza was a distant cousin of our mother. Only daughter of wealthy parents. In the year nineteen-o-five when she returned from her Swiss school, she was married to Sir Faridoon-jee Diamondcutter. He exported diamonds to Belgium.

Rodaba: After twenty-five years of their barren marriage he died. Lady Diamondcutter became a millionairess widow.

Homai: Hoshang Saroshyar Mirza was my childhood friend. His parents were ordinary people. His father was a bank clerk. How could he ever hope to marry the daughter of Sir Ardeshir Junkwallah? He received a scholarship from our educational trust and proceeded to England for higher studies, so that on his return, he could become somebody and be able to propose to me. In the meantime, we were ruined because of the Depression. My parents died. We became poor. In the year 1938 Hoshang come back from England, but he was unlucky as he had failed to secure a degree from the University of Cambridge. He could not get the kind of job he wanted. For three years he remained unemployed.

Homai: Then, one evening he said to me, standing right here in this window, "Homai dear, allow me to marry Lady Diamondcutter. She is old and ailing. Won't last long. She will conk out in a few years and we will get married. Both of us are facing hardships. This is the easiest way to solve our financial problem." I could not believe my ears, I was dumbfounded. He didn't wait for my answer, went out, crossed the lawn and entered Aunt Feroza's bungalow.

Rodaba: They were married in the firetemple. The wedding reception was held at the Turf Club. He became our Uncle Hoshang. Aunt Feroza couldn't believe her luck. In her old age she had married such a handsome young man.

Homai: Banam-i-Yazd—Now both Hoshang and I started waiting for her to pop off. At the time of her wedding she was sixty-plus. And Golchehr, I at that time must have been of your age! And Dara, Hoshang was very much like you! (*The young couple shudder and clasp each others' hands again.*)

Rodaba: But Aunt Feroza went on living. Sixty-five, seventy, eighty. And poor Hoshang was like her A.D.C. Aunt Feroza had ordered him not to meet us even on the quiet, or else she would leave all her wealth to some charity. She had engaged private detectives to spy on us.

Homai: So now Hoshang became desperate. He began blowing up her money. Race course. Cards. Drinks. Stock Market. She kept on giving him cheque after cheque of enormous amounts, to keep him happy.

Rodaba: By the time Aunt Feroza was eighty, Hoshang had made her almost bankrupt. He celebrated her 81st birthday with great fanfare. There were 18 candles on the eighteen-tiered cake. The best dance-band of Bombay played for the guests. We two watched the scene from this window.

Rodaba: Suddenly, we saw flames leaping up right in front of us. There was panic and tumult! Somebody came running to tell us that while Hoshang was lighting the candles, a curtain caught fire. I was sure Hoshang started the fire himself, he was so fed up. The fire-engines arrived. The wooden bungalow was burnt to cinders. Aunt Feroza survived even then. All the guests ran out.

Homai: Hoshang also saved himself. He ran away and disappeared. Some gatecrasher's corpse was found in the dining room entangled in the curtains. His face was half-burnt. The poor wretch resembled Hoshang. In her crazed state of mind Aunt Feroza thought it was Hoshang.

She immediately sent for an artist from the J.J. School and got his death-mask made. Then she had the last rites performed of the stranger. The press reported the news of 'the tragic death of Mr. Hoshang Saroshyar Mirza, who had not been able to escape from the inferno.'

Rodaba: (*Raises her forefinger and says conspiratorially*) But only we know the truth. The news was false. The world was mistaken. Aunt Feroza was mistaken. She still thinks that Hoshang died that night.

Homai: Her manor had turned to ashes. We two sisters were her only surviving relatives. After marrying Hoshang she had, for the last twenty years, stopped meeting us, but this was a catastrophe. We dutifully went across to offer our condolences. She was sitting on a chair under the laburnum tree, surrounded by some of her half-burnt expensive belongings. The death mask was in her lap. At that moment she looked like the terrible Goddess of Fate.

Rodaba: However, we had the last laugh. We requested her to shift to our house. She was known for her arrogance and imperious manners. She stared at us with anger and disdain. Then she pointed towards the death mask and said in her regal tone—Homai, Rodaba! This luckless man tried to get rid of me by starting the fire. He had thought that he would run away and I would die. While the guests were singing 'Happy Birthday' he vanished behind the crowd. I noticed him sneaking away with a couple of lighted candles. I followed him. He began setting fire to the curtains. I tried to stop him but before he could escape the burning curtains fell over him and the flames enveloped him.

Anyway, even now he hasn't been able to achieve his deliverance. His soul has left behind its imprint on this. Still she does not meet us. Every month she slips the envelope of the rent in our letterbox—

Homai: After some time the death mask was stolen from her bedroom. She had gone to the firetemple. On her return she found that it was missing. After the disappearance of the mask she has completely gone bonkers. (*Laughs aloud*) Dara! My Hoshang is very clever. He lives in Colaba in disguise. He spends his evenings at the Willingdon Club. On Saturday nights he sneaks in here to have dinner with us, and goes back to Colaba. (*The cuckoo clock strikes mine*).

Homai: There! He has come. (*Goes backstage*) *Rodaba sits down on the stool and begins playing "The Wedding March". After a few minutes Homai enters pushing a wheelchair. A figure made of wax, dressed in a black dinner suit is sitting erect in the wheelchair. The death mask of the late Hoshang Saroshyar Mirza has been fitted to the neck of the wax dummy. The ironic, dying smile of the departed is horribly petrified in plaster of paris.*)

(*Dara & Gulchehr scream "ya Ali!" and rush out. After a few moments the taxi starts and drives away, offstage. Rodaba is busy playing the `Wedding March'. Homai ties a napkin round the dummy's neck and places the wheelchair beside the dining table. Then she lights the candles on the dining table. Next, she switches off the electric lights.*)

Homai: (*Her back towards the sofa and the piano, placing a dish before the dummy*) Dara—Gulchehr— dinner is served, candlelight dinner—ever so romantic!

(*Rodaba begins playing the 'Fairy Waltz'. Homai is busy hovering over the dummy. Rodaba switches over to the 'Moonlight Sonata'. Then she abruptly gets up, comes towards the dining table. The sisters sit down opposite each other. The waxen Hoshang is in the middle. In the candlelight the three shadows look eerie on the wall. The sisters bend down their heads and whisper the Zoroastrian Grace.*) Ahur Mazda—who has

created the cow and the corn and trees and water—
May the angels Khordad and Amardad bless us with
each morsel— May this food be like honey and grant
us wisdom. May Evil and Sins be destroyed a thousand
times. (*Actual prayer in the Avestan language may be
recited here. Homai raises her head and turns towards
the sofa.*)

Homai: Dara, Gulchehr, come along, dear. Dinner is ready
. . . Good God— where are they? They have gone away.

Rodaba: Gone away? (*Pause*) Now I am wondering. *Who
on earth were those two?*

Homai: Never mind, Rudy. They must be mad. We asked
them to stay for dinner and they ran away in such foul
weather. Crazy foreigners. . .

Rodaba: Yes, dear. There is no dearth of batty people in
the world. One has to be very careful these days. All
manner of loonies can turn up to waste our time...
(*Suddenly laughs a horrible laugh*) Vanished
suddenly... were they ghosts. . .?

Homai: Crazy foreigners—loonies. Hoshang dear, have
the clear soup first—(*Takes out a spoonful of soup,
carries it to the death-mask's lips. The death-mask,
with its terrible smile, gets tilted over the plate. Outside,
rain and thunderstorm. Flash of lightning. Cats howl.
A gust of wind enters the window, and candles flicker
and blow out. The stage plunges into semi-darkness.
In the half-lights, Homai and Rodaba are seen putting
soup to the lips of the death mask as the curtain
slowly falls*).

7
Hyena's Laughter

T he valleys between the Himalayas and the Shivalik hills are known as "doons"—Dehra Dun being one of them. The Corbett National Park, spread over a hundred square miles, is located in one of the doons of the Nainital district. The Ram Ganga descends the mountains here and enters the Park. On the bank is the mountain range; on the other, the dense forest of *sal* trees. The forest is inhabited by tigers, leopards and the deer; the Ram Ganga by alligators who, unconcerned with our time, exist in the geological age of the dinosaurs, much like hippopotami and the elephants. Hearing the sound of a jeep on the forest road, the tigers, the leopards, and the antelopes suddenly disappear into the dense forest. One hears only the rustle of leaves or sees just a fleeting glimpse or a shadow—as if the disappearing animal were an idea hidden within the jungle of the human mind. Or sometimes, at night, one sees within the range of the headlights of a car or a jeep a hyena or an otter or a black bear—as if an unsuspected fear within one's own mind had suddenly materialised.

The forest is filled with the music of the deer, the colourful birds, the snakes, and the pitch-dark night; the silent symphony of the flowing river, the sleeping alligators, the birds and beasts, the snowy winters, the crawling mists and the darkness.

This year in December, all kinds of people were staying in the compound of the rest house at one end of the forest: a retired British army officer and his memsahib, travelling in their caravan car; a few students from the University of Cambridge come to study the flora and fauna in the Himalayas; and some European young men, all staying and sleeping in their camping tents. A little distance from them, in open tents, were a few workers and building contractors, busy putting up new buildings in the compound. The number of visitors to the Corbett National Park has increased steadily every year.

After dinner, the chief elephant man brought down all the elephants, who had been taught to bend down on their knees to greet the foreigners. The memsahibs fed every elephant a piece of bread. Then all living creatures went into their resting places—rooms, tents, huts, burrows, caves, nests, anthills—and to sleep until the next morning when the sun looked in on the Ram Ganga, and the forest and the compound woke up. Then each creature had his breakfast of goat meat, or live deer meat, or dead buffalo meat, or occasional human flesh, or raw meat, or worms and ants, or fried eggs, porridge and cornflakes, or toast and jam, jellies, marmalades and tea, or *puri bhaji* or dry bread or *parathas*, before starting his day.

And then quietly, on tiptoe, Buddhu, the pig, entered the compound. He would stand in front of the new building. The Rampuri waiter would shout: "Buddhu is here." Taking her walk on the road old Mrs. Freemantle would say, "Hello Boodoo, good morning!" and Brigadier Freemantle growl, "Hello, Boodoo, old rascal." The American tourists would smile and say, "Hi, Boodoo." And some American girl would exclaim, "Isn't he cute?"

Buddhu comes to the compound twice a day. He gets his breakfast and leaves; then he comes back for his supper and goes away again.

Evening. A green jeep wagon arrived during that misty evening and stopped in front of the new building. Two men and a young woman stepped out. The servants from the new rest house ran to haul their luggage in, for the visitors seemed affluent tourists, carrying a colourful, matching American-made suitcase, holdall, bag and an expensive picnic basket. The three of them entered the reception room which had a shiny bar in front. The girl raised her eyebrows and looked around in annoyance, as though the only hotels she ever went to were five-star hotels.

Brigadier Freemantle was sitting alone at the bar. One of the newcomers walked in, clad in Jodhpurs and a turban on his head, with one ear pierced, and sporting a sharp, pointed moustache. One still encounters such characters in the landscape of Rohilchand. He raised his finger to order "a brandy and soda" from the bartender— a young man from the northern hill country—and sat down on a crimson leather barstool. A few minutes later he noticed the Brigadier and tried to attract his attention. But the latter took no notice of him. Some Indians, in the presence of a white foreigner, often become very self-conscious. Immediately they slip into speaking English with an affected accent and seem proud to be talking to a white man. A curious meekness and humility takes possession of their entire demeanour. The Westerners on such occasions silently laugh at them. More often than not, these very Indians speak rudely to their own countrymen

The other newcomer was a thin, balding runt of a man, with hooded, listless eyeslike those of a slothwhich he moved about lackadaisically. He was talking in low tones to the manager of the rest house. The girl stood nearby, looking bored. She could have been a starlet or an expensive model—beautiful, fair-skinned, tall and healthy, with hazel eyes. She wore diamonds. The runt looked twice her age. A few minutes later they both went upstairs. The man with the pierced ear kept sitting at the bar drinking brandy. The roar of the tigers could be heard outside.

"What a shame that this wonderful tiger country is going to be drowned in the Kalagarh Dam," the man with the pierced ear commented.

"Yes, it is, isn't it?" the Brigadier responded briefly.

"I used to arrange hunts for the princes. Gone are those days. What about you?"

"I come here from England every year to do some fishing," the Brigadier answered.

"Can I be any service?" the man with the pierced ear inquired.

"No, thank you," the Brigadier said curtly.

Outside, the sounds of the night were becoming louder. A quarter of an hour passed. The man with the pierced ear stared at the Brigadier. One of his eyes was bloodshot. "The valley around is really very romantic," he said. "If you sometimes. . ."

This fellow is not one of those who just like to make small talk with the foreigners, the Brigadier thought and got up from the stool. He lit his cigar, said "Goodbye" and walked out rather quickly.

The man with the pierced ear began to drum with his fingers on the bar top. He finished his drink and asked the bartender for the number of his companion's room and then said, "Send the bill upstairs, to the sahib who was with the young lady. Which way is the staircase?"

The bartender told him.

Upstairs, he knocked at a door. From inside someone asked him to come in. The door was open. He walked in. The girl, reclining on the bed, was turning through the pages of Jim Corbett's *Man-Eaters of Kumaon,* a copy of which had been placed in every room for the benefit of the tourists. The runt lay on the other bed staring at the ceiling. He ordered, "Go now," in a voice that did not seem quite compatible with his meagre body.

"All right. I'll be out of Dhakala during the night. At Najibabad, you can . . ."

"Go," the runt interrupted him.

"Good night," he said to the girl. "I'll be back on Sunday morning. Be ready."

"Go," the runt repeated.

The man with the pierced ear bowed a farewell and went out.

The runt got up and opened one of the suitcases. He took out a whip and a leather belt and tossed the two towards the girl. Then he locked the door.

Early the morning Mrs. Freemantle was hanging up her laundry in front of her caravan car. Her husband sat in a chair nearby, reading the newspaper. Suddenly she said, "Poor girl. The poor thing!"

.The Brigadier kept quiet.

"The poor Indian child bride! Can we not to something for her, Henry?"

"What is it, Doris?" the Brigadier asked, a little peeved.

"That girl who came here last night, she was taking a walk this morning wrapped in shawl. There were whipping marks on her back under the sari. I think her husband flogs her. Can we not . . .?"

"Doris, don't poke your nose in other people's affairs."
"But, Henry. . . !"

At eleven in the morning, the girl stood in front of the mirror getting ready. She had put on a safari suit. The runt was a man of taste: while applying the Swiss pentane to the remnants of his salt-and-pepper hair, he broke into a joyful song: "In forest alone does the heart cheer/Love hungers after beauty there."

The girl listened to the song with attention.

"This is an old film song. Goes back before your time," he said, picking up his camera and binoculars.

Both came out and locked the door. Then they came down the stairs and went towards the platform for elephant rides. They climbed up the few stairs to the top of the platform and sat down in the howdah on the elephant's back. The elephant was waiting alongside the platform like an automobile.

In the howdah the girl burst out laughing. She was happy like a child. Her diamonds glittered in the sun. The mahout, a lanky man wearing a soiled khaki jacket, held the poker in his hand carefully and gently nudged the elephant, "Come on, daughter Ramkali, get going. In the name of God. . ."

Ramkali started towards the gate at an amble. Coming out of the compound, they passed through the farmland along the river and moved towards the forest. Excitedly and happily the girl looked all around through her binoculars, and time and again drew her companion's attention by saying, "Look, look, a peacock . . . a stag. Look there, an alligator. My God, how incredibly huge! Mahout, what animal is that one, over there?"

"An antelope, memsahib. But don't talk. The animals vanish as soon as they hear human voices."

Ramkali went into the thick forest. The nests of the weaverbird hung like chandeliers from the trees. From afar they saw two other elephants carrying the English students from Cambridge.

Having gone through one part of the forest, the trained Ramkali turned around. Reaching the rest house the girl tipped the mahout twenty rupees. Among the servants of the rest house, the girl had already acquired something of a reputation for her wealth and large-heartedness. One waiter, to please her, moved forward and pointed out, "Membsahib, look. Buddhu is here."

"Buddhu? Don't let him go. I"ll feed him myself today," she said and went in.

The dining hall was depressing. The girl, who had felt exhilarated in the forest, now sat down disheartened to have her meal.

At that time there was only one other family in the hall. Bored, she watched them. The wife's hair was oily, drawn back tightly into a bun; she was wearing a faded chintz nylon sari; she had gold bangles, vermilion in the partng in her hair and a blue plastic *bindi* on her forehead; all the children were dressed in readymade *baba* clothes; the husband sat with the latest issue of *Dharmyug* in his hands. Everyone seemed thoroughly sick of the others.

The waiter served her meal. He was a thin man from Rampur and resembled the well-known *tabla* player, Ahmad Jan Thirakwa. Life seemed such a colourless, shallow, embarrassing, absurd thing.

After the meal she brought out a plate of food for Buddhu, and later she went out for a walk along the river. On the way she met the woman with the plastic bindi, who looked her over critically. The girl smiled; the woman was obliged to smile back. The two began talking.

The woman asked, "What's your caste?"

"Brahmin," the girl replied.

"And what's your name?"

"Bandevi—the forest goddess," she said.

"Is that man your husband?"

"Who did you think he was?" the girl asked, cheerily. The woman moved on, frowning.

Coming out of the compound the girl came to the area where the construction workers had pitched their tents. They were putting up a new building. At that moment they were congregated at one edge of the forest, busy saying their prayer. Rich foods were cooking on open pits. One man, having finished the prayer asked, "Yes, mem sahib, what can we do for you?"

"Nothing, nothing. I was just passing by. What are you cooking here?"

"Why don't you give it a try? Hey, Dilawar, get some dessert for the mem sahib." He offered her the chair and continued talking, "We're from Bijnor. Have been here for a year, waiting for the project to finish. Only then can we return."

"Don't give her the dessert from the tray for the offering," one man said in low tones to Dilawar. The man had a white beard and looked very pious. The girl had overheard his comment.

Dilawar brought some yellow rice pudding in a flowered, enamelled dish. The girl smiled and asked, "Who was the offering for?"

"The Saint of Baghdad," Dilawar answered, a little embarrassed.

The girl tried a spoonful of the dessert and gave a twenty-rupee bill to Dilawar.

"Very kind of you, ma'am," the contractor said politely.

She bid goodbye to them and went back to the compound. The Bijnoris looked at each other in astonishment.

Eleven in the morning the third day. The Brigadier sat in the sun reading the newspaper. The runt came towards him in a rush and said, "I have to go to town on an urgent errand. I'll be back by nightfall or tomorrow morning. Would you and Mrs. Freemantle be kind enough to look after my wife?" Having said this he hopped into his jeep and drove out through the gate.

Mrs. Freemantle said, "The brute! Beats up a sweet and gentle girl like her. I'm sure her poor parents sold the pitiable thing to him for money. It's so common in the East."

Buddhu came and stood next to her chair. Mrs. Feemantle lovingly stroked his snout. Buddhu was a wild boar who used to emerge from the forest only for some entertainment and then go back. The people in the compound called him Buddhu (The Fool).

The girl came out of the rest house, said "Good morning," and sat in a chair.

"Boodoo," said the Brigadier, "is the best public relations officer of the forest, the animals' representative who maintains a liaison with the world of the human forest."

"Who knows what his forest is like?" the girl said.

"You've been in there, haven't you?"

"Yes, but not deep enough."

"It must seem the same to the animals as our world does to us. When we and the Japs were fighting in the forests of Burma, we both looked like beasts."

During the last two days, this sociable girl had become quite friendly with the English couple.

Mrs. Freemantle went towards the caravan car.

"Can I stay with you until lunch?" the girl asked the Brigadier.

"Of course. Even your husband asked us to . . ."

She giggled. "He's not my husband. I met him at the racecourse in Calcutta. He is a jockey and loaded with money. Has a wife and children. He is a pervert. I've been with him for the past six months and am tired of him now and want to leave but he wouldn't let me. I've squeezed more money out of him than I could have earned in a whole year. Look at these diamonds. Blue Belgium."

"Oh, I see," the Brigadier said. He was a man of the world. "But take care not to repeat any of this in front of my wife. She's an old-fashioned lady. She'll never speak to you again."

"Very well, Brigadier."

"But you look like a respectable girl from a decent family . . . ."

"Are you going to say what everybody else does: how come a nice girl like you is doing something like this? The answer to that, sir, is that there's big money in it. Actually, now our business is becoming international. Some of my colleagues have even been to the Middle East and the West already. My parents and brother know about it. They live in New Delhi."

"Who was that frightful chap who arrived with you?" the Brigadier inquired.

"My public relations man."

The Brigadier said gently, "But, my dear, don't you sometimes feel afraid? You might run into someone who is half insane or a sadist, or—there's really a very fine line between sanity and insanity."

"This man is a sadist too, but I know how to handle him. And in any case, there are always occupational hazards. One of my schoolmates became a nurse and went to Germany. There she gave up nursing and joined the Eros Palace in Hamburg. Within days she became a millionaire. Has a magnificent house, swimming pool, a beautiful car. If I get a chance, that's what I'm going to do."

"What are you going to do?" Mrs. Freemantle asked, returning from her caravan car.

"Social work, community service, Mrs. Freemantle," the girl answered with firmness.

"Really!" the Brigadier said under his breath.

A little later she left for lunch. In the afternoon she came out on the porch. A wounded bird, flapping his wings, hit a doorpost and fell down. The girl picked it up and began stroking it out of real sorrow and compassion. Suddenly she had an idea. She hid the bird under the edge of her sari and went off towards the camp of the Cambridge students.

The five of them were sitting in front of small, open tent. Three boys and two girls. The young men were healthy, tall, golden haired, golden bearded, the gods of the northern forests of Europe, progeny of the sun god; the girls milk-white, blonde and fresh-looking, the goddesses of the forest. How magnificent these Europeans looked, she thought. On the other hand, we Indians are so grubby, dark, emaciated, deformed and ugly; such miserable runts; mere insects—crickets and grasshoppers. She kept watching the five of them fondly. Then hesitating, she moved a little closer to them. They were busy discussing some issue. The books on their subjects lay near them.

"Good afternoon," she said. "Excuse me!"

"Hello. Good afternoon," one golden-haired god approached her.

She offered him the wounded sparrow. "You people are studying the life in the forest. I thought you might be interested," she said.

"Oh! How very nice of you. Thanks." The boy cupped the bird carefully in his hands and hurried towards his companions. They immediately began tending to the bird's injuries.

For a few minutes she stood there waiting, hoping that they would strike up a conversation with her. Then, disappointed, she went back to the compound.

In the evening, as she stood weary and bored in the patio, she spotted the same English boy going towards the bar. She rushed inside and seated herself in a sofa. The boy bought some bottled beer and walked towards the door. She waved at him and said hello. He smiled with a slight bow and came towards her.

"Good evening, ma'am. . . Mrs. . .?"

"Mrs. Ale."

"How are you, Mrs. Ale?"

"My name is Rum."

"Ale and Rum—you're pulling my leg?"

"No, I'm not. I call my husband Ale. He has become known by that name. My real name is Rumbha who in Hindu mythology is a celestial dancer."

"How interesting!" the boy said. "My name is simply Bernard Craig."

"Sit down, Bernard. Have a coffee with me." She called the waiter. Suddenly she looked happy and hopeful. "How's your bird now?" she asked.

"He became well after we bandaged him up. Flew back to his woodland." The body sat down and began making small talk with her.

"I think we too should go back to our jungle, that is, the civilised world. It's not easy to spend time here. Time is so stationary here. But the captain wants to stay on for a few more days and go on the big hunt, at the foot of the mountains where the Ram Ganga begins."

"We too came here to visit the places where the rivers begin," the sun god said. A halo of golden hair, golden beard, luminous like the sun itself in the dim light of the bar.

She didn't take her eyes off him. He was saying, "I like India so much that I'm almost tempted to marry some Indian girl. My friends in England who have Indian wives are very happy. They say you people prove to be very loyal and obliging wives, quite unlike the English girls."

She blushed, feeling restless.

The waiter brought the coffee and she got busy pouring it into the cups. Then she asked him, "Have you seen any tiger yet?"

"No. The trap was set the day before yesterday. We waited on the scaffold for quite some time, but the tiger didn't show up. In two or three days we'll be in New Delhi, and then it's back to England."

The girl began to talk in a low, sad voice. "My father, His Highness of Karanpur, was a well-known hunter of his time. I've been on many big-game hunts with him. My brother is also an expert hunter."

The young Englishman was listening to her with fond attention. She continued: "When the princedoms here were abolished, I was very small. It changed our entire way of life. When I grew up I had to become an air hostess." She lifted her hand to show him the ring. "This blue Belgium is the last relic of our family treasure."

"Fascinating! So you were a flying princess!"

"It was during one of my flights that I struck up a friendship with the captain. We got married. He started drinking heavily, so he was grounded. He has become intolerable. Now, I'm in the process of getting a divorce from him. I wish . . ."

The young man kept quiet.

"This place is part of nature. Here one is obliged to speak the truth. That's why I'm telling you all this."

"I am honoured, Mrs. Ale," he said gently.

A man clad in a heavy black overcoat walked into the room. Bernard observed him and said, "Mrs. Ale, have you ever wondered how some people resemble animals? For example, doesn't this man look like a Himalayan bear? And yesterday we saw a tiny fellow. He looked exactly like a sloth."

"And what animal do I look like?" the girl asked smiling.

The boy looked at her probingly and said, "A leopard . . . or a lynx maybe . . ."

"Thanks. Because of my eyes? Yes, there is a lot common between human and animal eyes. The badger has unlucky eyes; fish have cold eyes and the ox has stupid eyes."

"Look there, an ibex just jumped on to the barstool," the boy said jovially.

She too laughed. "Some people look like frogs, others like elephants or rhinos or grasshoppers or cattle or herons. Some women look like geckos, or silly sparrows."

"We're all in the same family," Bernard said. "A Hindu friend of mine tells me that all living creatures are a family and according to the theory of the transmigration of souls each has to go through eighty thousand incarnations.

"Really?" the girl asked surprised.

"You're not a Hindu?"

"My mum, Her Highness of Kiranpur, was a Christian."

"Oh!" Bernard gave her a long and deep look. He finished his coffee and stood up. "Thanks for the coffee. Good night, Princess. See you tomorrow!"

He walked out a little quickly and disappeared in the mist.

The fourth morning the Cambridge students were busy studying in the shade of a tree. She walked by them, but they did not see her. ("I'm almost tempted to marry some Indian girl. I'm almost tempted . . . .") Walking quickly she reached the tents of the Bijnoris. The old man with the radiant face sat on a prayer rug.

"*Assalamo alaikum!*" she uttered the Muslim form of greeting.

"*Walaikumus salam!*" the old man responded but observed her a little suspiciously.

In a pleading tone, she spoke slowly, "Sir, pray for me. Pray to your saint for me. Beg him to show me some favour so that my life gets on the right course. Please, please. Do something quickly. Here, take it," she took out two hundred-rupees bills from her purse, placed them in front of him and returned. The old man sat there, bewildered, watching her.

The runt was back by evening; he was standing on the porch supervising the loading of the fishing gear into the jeep. He ordered a porter, "Go, tell the mem sahib to hurry up!"

The porter went upstairs and knocked at the door. She was dressed in a grey trouser-suit and stood before the mirror putting on her make-up. She opened the door and asked the porter to reassure the sahib that she'd be down soon. Then clambering down the back stairs she ran towards the Cambridge students' camp.

Bernard was sitting on a stone under a banyan tree, smoking his pipe. Surprised he said, "Good evening, Mrs. Ale."

"Rum," the girl corrected him, smiling.

He kept quiet. He didn't want to complicate his life by getting involved with a married woman.

"I'm not Mrs. Ale." She seemed deeply troubled. "Please give me your address in New Delhi. I want to get out of this mess. I'd like to go to Britain. Will you help me?"

"This is absurd. Every Indian I meet wants me to help him get to Britain," he answered sourly.

"I'll tell you the whole story. Everything. Just give me your address in New Delhi."

"We haven't decided yet where we're going to stay in New Delhi."

The jeep came and stopped near her and the runt asked her coldly to get in. Flustered she looked at Bernard and then got into the jeep. Near the gate the jeep got stuck in the sand. Brigadier Freemantle was strolling nearby. He called a few men. Together they gave the vehicle a push, and it went out of the gate. The girl looked back. The Brigadier wiped his face and balding pate with his handkerchief and waved her goodbye. Lights were lit in the students' camp in the distance.

It was pitch dark on the way to the woods. Frightened, she slid closer to him. "It's very scary here. Go back to the rest house . . ." she said.

"Tomorrow, that hunt-guide brother of yours is coming back. Is that why you've asked him to come? I'll see how you leave!"

She thought: I'm not going with him either. Right now the bearded old man will be saying a prayer for me. Mrs. Bernard Craig. I'm determined to prove a dutiful, loyal wife. If that doesn't work, then the Eros Palace in Germany. "Stupid ass," she heard the voice of the man with the pierced ear. She imagined him sitting on the scaffold with a gun in hand, and she was tied up on the ground like a trapped goat, waiting to lure a tiger. She thought again of the Bijnori old man's radiant face and felt light-hearted, safe and happy. She said to the runt, "Sing us that song again."

He acted as if someone had just placed a needle on a record, immediately starting to sing:

"In the forest alone does the heart cheer

Love hungers after beauty there
Here people drink from the cup of love
The strangers don't know what love is about
We can't make a song
That opens the blossom of a heart
My heart never blossomed before..."

He parked the jeep on the sand. She jumped down and began helping him bring out the fishing gear.

The Ram Ganga glittered like molten silver. The man took out his hip flask and took a swig.

"It's even colder here," the girl said, shivering.

"What did you expect on a December night on the river bank? A heat wave?" the man answered. "Take a jog. It'll drive the cold away."

She started jogging on the sand. He too followed her at a terrier's trot. But he soon sat down panting. Suddenly startled by the scene before her, the girl exclaimed, "Oh, what a beautiful place!" She took off the strap of the coffee flask from her shoulder and plopped down on the sand.

Across from her, on the other side of the river, a hill belonging to the Shivalik range stood like a stone wall. The light reflecting from the water shimmered on the walls of a cave cut by the current of the river. It looked like the palace of the water nymphs. The man plonked down next to her. He put the hip flask to his lips and, a little tipsily, began purring and waxing poetic: "On the bank of the river, in a moonlit night, a drink in your hand, your lover close by; a loaf of bread, a jug of wine; come on, have a sip, love."

"No, I'll have coffee." Then she said to herself: Maulvi sahib, the bearded cleric, would be saying a prayer for me at this very moment. How can I be sitting here drinking?

He rambled on: "My lover close by, my stupid lover, my black-guard, rascally lover,. . ." and downed the whole flask. He sat there looking like a mouse whose insides were full of molten lead. He shut his eyes: his head was falling forward.

The girl grumbled, "Is this the time or the season for fishing? Come on, take me back, or I'm going to die of pneumonia."

He was lost to her.

"I'm going to go sit in the jeep," she said.

He did not stir.

"Orangutan!"

No movement.

"Badger!"

Still no movement.

"Insect! Midget!"

He kept quiet.

"Doddering old grasshopper."

Suddenly he stood up and gave her a hard kick. She slipped and fell into the water.

"Help! Help! Save me!" she screamed. The receding current carried her deeper into the water. Across, the image of the cave trembled on the water. An alligator, awakened from its prehistoric, timeless sleep, slowly slid down the rock. Entering the water it moved towards the drowning girl.

Scrambling furiously, the girl raised her head above the surface. She saw that the water, glistening in the cool light of the moon, was all around her, and a black alligator, its jaws wide open, was advancing towards her.

The alligator grabbed the girl's legs in its jaws. She uttered a deafening scream. Then there was silence. The girl had died of the dread even before going into the alligator's mouth.

Holding her in its jaws, the alligator swam towards the cave. It rested for a second under the stone wall. At that moment it was alive in a bygone age of the earth, as were the Himalayan rivers issuing from the snow, the mountains, the forests, the rocks. The alligator started dismembering the girl's body and devouring her. A few tiny eddies of blood appeared on the surface of the water, and clumps of hair and pieces of flesh and torn clothes began floating above. Calmly and unhurriedly the alligator was having his dinner.

The runt saw all this from the bank. The hair on his body and head stood on end. With fear, his sloth's listless eyes popped wide open and stayed open. Panic-stricken he ran towards the jeep that stood near an old tree, far from the bank. The trunk of the thick tree, eaten up by the white ants, had snake pits in it. The leaves rustled with the commotion. A boa constrictor peeped out of the pit, and a doe woke up. Shaking, the man turned to look behind him: the Ram Ganga was peaceful, flowing like molten silver. He started the engine. The rumble of the engine was horrifying in that silence. Blindly racing the jeep, he came back on the forest road. Suddenly, a hyena came smack in front of the headlights and laughed loudly.

The night passed. The moon had set. The sun appeared on the Ram Ganga. The forest awoke. At breakfast time, Buddhu came out of the trees into the compound. He came under the porch of the rest house and stood there, his head bowed, waiting for the girl who used to feed him every morning.

Translated by Faniq Hassan
and Muhammad Umar Memon

8
The Missing Photograph

D ularey Mian was a gentle, refined and good natured young man who belonged to the small gauge branch line. It did not mean that he worked for the small gauge Rohilkhand Kumaon Railway whose very romantic toy train chugged its way through tiger-country and disappeared in the Himalayan foothills. The phrase "Chhoti Line" in our family parlance signified that Dularey Mian mother was an "outsider". There was at least one Dularey in every feudal family of north India. If some wayward man with a lot of unearned income from the agricultural lands had a concubine or two tucked away in secret hideouts, their children were referred to as small gauge branch-line, after their father's death. They become "second-class-citizens" as it were, not exactly servants and not quite full-fledged relatives. However, they were graciously absorbed in the commonwealth of the joint family. They were employed as caretakers of the mango-orchards or *karindas* who collected land revenue from the peasants. Out of sheer courtesy and good manners no one ever mentioned their origin. The girls were usually married off to members of similar "branch lines" existing in the network of landed gentry. In their old age these people were given as much respect as other elders in the family.

Dularey Chacha was a distant relative of ours. He was not the illegitimate son of a mistress. His father had properly married a *meerasin* or a woman of the musician caste.

Meerasins were not courtesans. They were genteel purdah-observing housewives who sang only in the *zenanas* or ladies apartments during weddings, childbirth, and other festivities. Their menfolk were sometimes famous *ustads* or maestroes of Hindustani classical music. They were greatly honoured by their patrons as performing artistes, but no one could dream of marrying his daughter to a *meerasi*, however celebrated he might be as a singer or instrumentalist. And no one could dare marry in a *meerasin* family. All this was part of the old world culture. The class structure was such that a *meerasin* could not sit on the same divan with the *begums*—women of rank. So how could she become one of them?

The Arabic world *meeras* means inheritance. Hindustani classical music was the cherished and ardently preserved heritage of the *meerasis.* They married within their own caste or families of distinction called *gharanas.* Their women were not properly taught music. They simply imbibed it from their male relatives. On the other hand courtesans diligently learned classical music and dance from the ustads. Nawabs and Rajahs kept some of these courtesans in their harems, even married them.

Our family, like hundreds of others like us, was part feudal and part "service and professional gentry," who were also absentee landlords. In fact, the latter had come into existence over the debris of pre-1857 feudal structure. As Syeds, they were obsessed with the maintenance of the purity of the Blood Sublime—being descendants of the Prophet on *both* sides. Our family bhats had memorised the impeccable genealogy which was recited generation after generation at the time of the son's weddings. The marriages were usually celebrated in the *qasba* and the entire extended family gathered for it from all over the country.

It was at the marriage of my uncle, just before the First Word War, when one of the kinsmen fell head over heels in love with an attractive *meerasi* he had seen dancing the "Ghungat-ka-Naach" in the zenana. He quietly married her and thus impaired the purity of his lineage. It was unforgivable.

His wife was now neither fish nor fowl—neither a *meerasin* nor quite a begum. And her children would be second-class or lower-grade Syeds.

Dularey was their only child. His parents died when he was quite young. Despite his being of "the Chhoti Line" he endeared himself to the whole clan because of his sweet temperament. He inherited his father's estate and began to live lavishly and in great style. He was a college dropout, though not a playboy. He did not drink or gamble. His one harmless passion was Indian movies.

Dularey Mian was immensely popular in our *qasba*. He was helpful and generous. In the mango season he invited the entire clan to his orchard where he hosted a sumptuous lunch followed by mangoes plucked fresh from the trees and dumped in tubs full of iced water. Dularey was also very fond of shikar and often went big-game hunting in the foothills with his friends and hangers-on. Being a zamindar in his own right, Dularey was not treated as poor relation. Still, he could not hope to marry in the 'clan' or the endogamous family because he was not a pure, high-born Syed; he had *meerasi* blood in him.

His house stood across the lake, surrounded by his own green fields and orchards. He had a Ford motor car which he drove down to the nearby town and saw the latest "talkie" every week. Whenever we went to our *qasba*— myself, my brother and our cousins—we loved to visit him and hear his shaggy dog stories and shikar anecdotes. He always had stacks of gifts ready for us—air guns, Meccano sets and footballs for the boys, English dolls, Gollywogs (we did not know that it was a highly racist toy) and fancy embroidery kits for us, little females. And heaps of chocolates. He doted on us.

Sometimes he told us of the silent movies of his youth. "I saw Sulochane's *Telephone Girl* four times. She is a beautiful Jewess from Austria, you know. Her real name is Ruby Mayers."

Once he gave me a Nestle's Album full of Hollywood stars' pictures which came with the chocolates. Then he added proudly. "See, there are two Indian film stars included in this lot—Seeta Devi and Indira Devi. Seeta Devi's real name is Renee Smith."

His knowledge of films was truly encyclopaedic—"*Shiraz* was made by Himansu Roy in 1929. With German cooperation. Germans are fantastic people, you know. They lost the war—but they continue to be leaders in science—And in *The Light of Asia* Himansu Roy had played the Buddha himself. The film was seen by the King and Queen and the entire Royal Family. It ran for four months in London."

We listened to all this, wide-eyed. "And in *Karma* Devika Rani sang in English—Karma—Karma—"

Absolutely fascinating.

Then he had piles of publicity pamphlets distributed by funny-looking men carrying megaphones, before the release of a film. The leaflets carried pictures of fantasy ladies: Madhuri, Miss Bibbo, Jehan Ara Kajjan, Miss Gohar. Annual numbers of Urdu literary magazines also published their pictures. They wore their hair in "puff" fashion. Their blouses were quaint and their saris had frills and bows stitched on them as borders. They reclined on couches or stood languidly against fake marble columns and looked utterly out of this world. There was a photograph of one lady called Mukhtar Begum. She was smoking a cigarette.

"She is the prima donna of Urdu stage and a source of inspiration for Agha Hashr Kashmiri, the Indian Shakespeare," we were told.

We could not comprehend this bit about Mukhtar Begum being the source of inspiration for playwright Agha Hashr, but we kept quiet because Dularey Chacha had already proceeded to inform us about the Beauty Queen, Nasim Bano. "Her mother's name is Shamshad Bai. Once Lawrence of Arabia attended her mehfil in Delhi—while he was going about in disguise."

"Lawrence of Arabia!" we chorused in awe. Then an inquisitive and observant cousin returned to Mukhtar Begum—

"Look, she is smoking."

"I know," I replied knowledgeably. "All bad women smoke."

"Who told you that?" Dularey Chacha asked.

"Well, everybody says so."

"Women started smoking in the West after the World War, as a symbol of equality with men. In our society, unfortunately, smoking is associated only with women of the show business. They couldn't care less as they have no reputation to lose," he said carefully.

We were too young to realise at that time that Dularey Chacha was socially conscious as well, and that he secretly sympathised with the Indian Bolsheviks led by M.N. Roy.

Imtiaz Ali Taj, a young family friend in Lahore, had joined what was called the Avant Garde of India.It included celebrities like Amrita Shergill, Baldoon Dhingra, Patras Bokhari, etc. Taj had made an art film called *Sohag Ka Daan.* It starred Anwar Bai of Amritsar. Dularey-cha was very excited.

He told my mother, "Bhabhi Saheb, what a film Taj Mian has made. When the Mantri says— *Maharani,tumharey sohag par mrityu ki chhaya kanp rahi hai—*"[1]

"Dularey, I wish you had pursued your college studies with the same concentration with which you memorise film dialogue," my mother cut him short sternly.

Dularey-cha kept quiet. He looked crestfallen. I felt very bad. He was so sweet. Why did everybody silently disapprove of him?

His well-furnished lounge displayed framed photographs of Zubeida, Sultana, Devika Rani, Sabita Devi, Kanan Bala, etc. Their saris were sprinkled with zinc powder and when the chandeliers were lighted the picture twinkled in a row. One frame was, however, empty. We children had been told never to ask him about that missing photograph. So we didn't. Thereby hung a tale.

It transpired that as a young man Dularey Chacha had visited Bombay with his cronies and went to the film studios to meet his favourite stars. There this famous actress fell in love with him. She told him that she was very unhappy in her life of ill-repute. She yearned to attain respectability as a married woman. Out of sheer goodness of his heart he said "What the hell!", married her within a week, and brought her home. Of course, nobody in the family condescended to meet her.

Dularey Chacha endured this insult and took her to Mussoorie for "The Season". That was the year when three top film actresses of Bombay were staying in a row of bungalows as His Highness the Nawab of Rampur's guests. Dularey Chacha was no nawab, but he felt greatly pleased— he had even married a noted actress.

We lived in Dehra Dun. One Sunday afternoon, as I stood under a leechi tree, watching the squirrels run up and down, I saw a tonga enter the gate. Dularey Chacha sat in the backseat in his aristocratic manner, dressed in

---

1. The Shadow of death is flickering over your sohag— (husband"s life).

a black sherwani, white churidar pyjamas, and he wore Saleemshahi shoes of gold threadwork. A darkish woman in a red georgette sari sat by his side. I ran down to the portico and greeted him happily, "Adaab, Dularey-cha." Then I salaamed the lady. She smiled radiantly and said, "Jeeti rahiye[2], Bitiya." Both got down from the tonga. He said, "Bibi, go and tell Bhabhi Saheb, that Dularey has come. He has brought his wife for her *qadambosi[3].*"

Now, that was the courtly, formal Urdu language. *Qadambosi* did not mean that they were literally going to kiss my mother's feet. I rushed in.

Amman was in her bedroom. She was one of the early feminists of India and also a famous novelist of her time. She played the sitar and drove a car, but perhaps even she was not willing to meet a fallen woman. She said sullenly— "I'm sorry. I have high blood pressure, as he knows well, and Dr. Hoon has ordered complete bed rest. No visitors."

In later years I often wondered why she did that, but somehow always forgot to ask her. I knew she was deadly against bigamists and refused to meet them. But Dularey Chacha had committed no bigamy. Despite her liberation, perhaps she, too, could not socially accept an actress.

I went back to the front verandah and rather sheepishly repeated the message. Dularey Chacha looked grief-stricken. Obviously he had not expected this from such an enlightened person as my Amman. His wife quietly placed a big cardboard box, containing an English doll, on the edge of the verandah. They climbed back in the tonga and left.

On his return from Dehra Dun he must have felt so heartbroken that he didn't even take her to his *haveli* in the village. He went straight to the foothill where he had a hunting lodge in his own forest. The lady lived there in seclusion.

In those days there was no film press, no gossip columns. Cinema had not become a colossus and it had not captured the psyche of the Indian nation. So the marriage of a movie actress and her disappearance from the scene was hardly noticed.

---

2. May you live long.
3. Kissing the feet.

Times changed rapidly. Khurshid Mirza, daughter of
the founders of Aligarh Muslim Girls College, joined the
Bombay talkies as Renuka Devi. Her parents were close
friends of my father and Amman. Being a married woman,
like Devika Rani, Renuka Devi also had a social sanction.
"Well, her husband has allowed her," was the general
comment. Earlier Uzra and Zohra, from an aristocratic
family of Rampur, had joined Uday Shankar's troupe.
There was no uproar; they too had their family's sanction
and, anyway, they belonged to the upper strata of society.
So it was also a matter of class. Renuka Devi's sister-in-
law became "Mysterious Neena", followed by Begum Para,
the "Oomph Girl", also from Aligarh Muslim Girls College.

Dularey-cha's wife had no social backing. She served
him hand and foot and spent her time in *namaz-roza*
(prayer and fasting). Off and on he came to his house in
the *qasba*. He had taken off her framed photograph from
his "picture gallery". After a couple of years, his wife died
of jaundice. It is said that she was very happy that she
was to be buried as a respectable married woman. It was
said that a *sohagin* who died in her husband's lifetime
was very fortunate indeed. She was buried by the side of
her "outcaste" mother-in-law.

Dularey Chacha returned to the village and occupied
himself in his old pastimes, which now also included
writing of doleful Urdu poetry.

After Partition most of the "clan" migrated to Pakistan.
The abolition of Zamindari made Uncle Dularey a pauper
overnight. He had lived luxuriously in the traditional
Zamindari style and had not saved a paisa. Now he started
selling his mango orchards, valuables and heirlooms and
continued to be a good host and a helpful friend.

A few years ago I happened to visit my literally deserted
village. It was full of ruins of our ancestral houses and
new, overpopulated slums. I found Dularey Chacha in his
dilapidated *haveli*, still sitting in the same arm chair,
smoking his *pechawan*. He was pleased to see me. The
house looked empty. The chandliers had been sold. The
carpets had disappeared. The photographs of the actressess
were hanging askew, covered with dust and cobwebs.
Birds had built their nests behind Leela Desai and "Leela
Chitnis B.A." There was immense sadness in the air. He

asked me about various relatives. I told him about the members of the extended family who were now living in post-partition diaspora—in Pakistan, England, Europe and North America. Some of the boys had married women of many western nations. One girl settled in England had married a non-Muslim. The Blood Sublime had not remained very pure, anyway. He listened to my narration very calmly and said without any rancour or irony, "The last of your family *bhats* is still around. You must meet him, too. He is old and unemployed, because there are no genealogies left for him to recite. They have all gone away."

"Yes. Dularey-Cha. I met him. He told me his sons did not like to be called *bhats.* They have become truck drivers in the Gulf countries and he also informed me that Sarwari, the last of our family *meerasins* had also died—"

Then I bit my tongue. I had dropped a brick. Apparently, Dularey Chacha was past caring. He continued puffing at his hookah. I hastily took up his favourite subject—Films—

"You know, Sultana's daughter has married a Pakistani cricketer."

"Yes. yes. Sultana, she married Razzak Bawla whose brother was murdered on Malabar Hill because of Mumtaz Begum. She went away to Hollywood." For a moment he had become Dularey Chacha of our golden childhood.

"Did people go to Hollywood in those days too?" I asked surprised.

"Why? Was it an antedeluvian age? Are your times the best?" He turned towards his water-pipe. He seemed hurt by my remark. He must have been over 75 and looked much older. Obviously he was not getting enough to eat.

Then I glanced at the heroes in the second row of pictures—Gul Hamid, Raja Sandow, E. Billimoria, Master Vithal, Motilal, Master Nisar. There was a time when Dularey-cha looked like one of them with his razor-thin moustaches, polka-dot scarves and pork-pie hats.

I had taken with me some glossy film magazines for him.

"Bibi, I can't see very clearly, because of my cataract," he said calmly.

I didn't give up my attempt to cheer him up. I said, "Dularey-cha, this is a new actress from London. Her mother was the heroine in *Shahjehan.*"

"Yes, yes, Nasreen acted in *Shahjehan*," he said half-sitting up. "Anwar Bai of Amritsar's daughter." A faint glint of memory appeared in his dim eyes. "Her father was Rafique Chaznavi, the music director. In 1947. Anwar Bai married Jugal Kishore Mehra, Prithviraj's brother-in-law. He was a friend of Taj Mian. His motorcar was sent every week to fetch Anwar Bai from Amritsar to Lahore for the shooting of *Sohag-Ka-Daan*."

He paused a little and muttered, *"Maharani, tumhare shoag par mrityu ki chhaya kaanp rahi hai."* His voice trailed off and he bent down his head sleepily. I made a valiant effort to bring him up-to-date in the affairs of Anwar Bai. I said, "Mr. Mehra had a metamorphosis. He became Sheikh Ahmed Salman, Director General, Radio Pakistan. Then Anwar Bai's son-in-law went to U.K. and made a lot of money in carpets. Now Anwar Bai lives in a huge country house in England."

I realised that Uncle Dularey was not listening. He was not interested in the Present. I looked around again and noticed the ancient gramophone in a corner. There was a box of old 76 R.P.M. records, kept on a sidetable. I picked up a record and put it on the disc. Suddenly Mukhtar Begum began to groan—*Jin bolo Tara Tara*[4]. It was quite eerie.

Mukhtar Begum (who smoked) had been a friend of Dularey Cha's late wife. A bird fluttered its wings and flew out from behind Ratan Bai's picture. The space next to Ratan Bai was still empty. Long ago Dularey Chacha had taken off the photograph of his wife, hoping that society would accept her. He had been disappointed. The gramophone was broken, too. Mukhtar Begum continued to sing off key—*Jin bolo Tara, Jin bolo Tara, Tara*—

Dularey Chacha had started snoring. It was the anxiety-ridden, tired sleep of lonely old age. I came out of the haveli as the splintered stained glass of its once imposing front doors glimmered in the fading sunset.

P.S. A few days ago somebody informed me that Dularey Chacha had passed away. He was buried by the side of his mother and wife—both had been rejected by his own people. The haveli was occupied by a Main Line relative. He rented its spacious lounge to a political party for its local office. Chander Mohan, Prithviraj, K.L. Sehgal, and the rest were replaced by the mug-shots of the party boss and his fierce-looking henchmen.   ☐☐☐

---

4. Don't call me Tara, Tara!